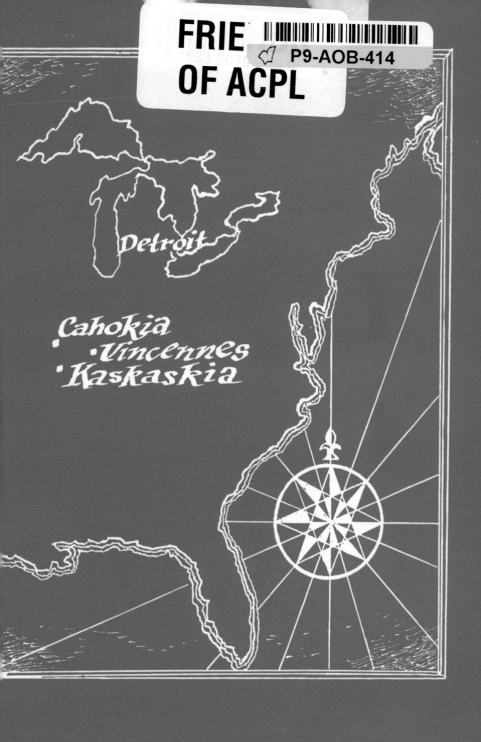

Detroit

Cahokia
•Vincennes
•Kaskaskia

JIM LONG-KNIFE

Minnemung

JIM LONG-KNIFE

By Florance Walton Taylor

Illustrated by
Dirk Gringhuis

ALBERT WHITMAN & COMPANY

Chicago   Illinois

DEDICATION
To Alan's three little queens;
Elizabeth,
Leslie,
Sarah.

Permission is gratefully acknowledged for the use
of material from "George Rogers Clark Papers" in
Vol. 8 of the *Collections* of the Illinois State Histori-
cal Library, edited by James Alton James, copyright
1912.

TABLE OF CONTENTS

Chapter I

A STRANGE GUEST

Thirteen-year-old Jim Hudson thumped a melon with practiced fingers, then pulled it from the vine and laid it in a pile with the others. He wiped his hot forehead with his sweaty shirtsleeve, turning with a smile toward his mother. "Look, Ma!" he called, "See how many melons we have. And how fine the turnips and corn look."

Ma Hudson, her rifle across her knees, was sitting on a large stump in the little clearing. She turned at the sound of Jim's voice, and smiled wearily at her towheaded boy. "Yes, Jim. We'll have plenty to eat this winter, I'm thinking."

Jim moved on to another vine and glanced along the row to where his father was kneeling. Ma pushed her sunbonnet back over her faded yellow hair and resumed her watch into the wilderness surrounding the clearing.

All during the spring and summer the Hudsons had worked in this fashion. Jim and Pa had planted their crops and enlarged the clearing by felling trees, while Ma had sat ready with the Kentucky rifle, and looked for hostile Indians.

This year of 1777 was a fearful one for Kentucky settlers. Some had been captured or killed by Indians; others had returned to Virginia discouraged by repeated Indian attacks. The Hudsons, however, had not been molested and Pa Hudson was determined to stay on his land. It was the first farm he had ever owned; he loved every inch of this lush Kentucky wilderness. He and Jim continued to gather melons. Jim worked faster than his father, because each time Pa moved from one vine to another, he had to pick up his rifle lying close by on the ground.

Suddenly Jim raised his head and listened. Then he turned to his father. "Pa, I hear something groaning. Do you?"

Pa seized his rifle and was on his feet immediately. "Where, son?"

Jim cocked his head toward the right. "Over there. Listen. There it is again."

At this moment Ma Hudson called, "Pa, I hear groaning." She was already picking her way among the stumps toward the sound, the rifle grasped firmly in her hands.

Pa went striding through the melon patch. "Wait, Ma. Let me go first." Soon he was ahead of her, with Jim beside him.

The three made their way through the tangled brambles into woods so dense the Hudsons seemed to be walking in twilight. Quite suddenly they saw a bridled horse standing quietly just ahead of them. In a moment the groaning sound came again, this time to the left of where Jim was standing.

He whirled around, scrambled over a large fallen tree and cried, "Why, here's a boy! Kind of a small boy, too." Jim started to stoop down toward the prostrate form.

Pa sprang to his side. "Wait a minute, son." He peered through the gloom and saw an Indian boy smaller than Jim, dressed in a long blue cloth shirt, his face streaked with hideous vermilion. "Maybe this is a trick," Pa muttered. "Perhaps he's been put here to lure us into a trap." Holding his rifle ready, Pa started looking about in the shadowy woods.

Ma Hudson's hands trembled as she held her rifle and looked down at the boy. "Pa, he's hurt. Look at his shoulder. This is no trick."

Pa handed his rifle to Jim. "You watch with Ma, while I have a look at him." He dropped to his knees to examine the boy, mumbling, "I'm still afraid it's an Indian trick."

As Pa turned the boy to one side, he saw an ugly wound

where the blue shirt was torn from one shoulder. Then he looked closely at the wound. "Why, I can see a bone too, Ma. I think he's broken his shoulder."

Ma forgot about the possibility of other Indians lurking near, as she ventured closer to Pa to look at the boy again. "Pa, he's not as old as Jim. We'll have to take care of him. We can't leave him here."

"No, reckon we can't," Pa replied, as he tried to lift the Indian boy from the tangled underbrush. But the boy's body was enmeshed in a stout wild grapevine. Pa took out his long knife and began slashing at the tangled vine.

At this moment, the Indian boy groaned and opened his eyes. He looked up at the Hudsons in alarm. When he saw Pa's long knife, he was terrified and cried out, *"Shemolsea! Shemolsea!"*

"What did you say?" Jim asked, but the boy had lost consciousness again.

When Pa had freed the boy from the vine, he gathered him in his arms and turned to Jim. "You go ahead with the rifle, Jim, and Ma, you walk behind me. Mind you both keep a sharp lookout. We'll have to take him back to the cabin."

"But Pa," put in Jim, "what'll we do about the horse?" He nodded toward the animal standing a few feet away.

"Bring him along. And tie him up in our lean-to next to Nellie. But not too close to our horse. She might nip him."

The Hudsons took the boy and his horse back to their cabin without seeing another human being. While Jim tethered the horse at a safe distance from Nellie, Ma flew about the cabin getting water, her home-made soap, and clean rags for Pa. He set the wounded boy's broken bone as best he could, supporting it with a rude splint. Then with Ma's help, he washed the wound with soap and bound the shoulder with rags to hold the bone securely in place.

When they had finished Pa shook his head. "I'm afraid he's lost a lot of blood. He'll be a while getting well."

Ma turned to Jim who was standing in the doorway of the cabin. "Jim, we'll have to put him in your bed. He's awfully weak."

Jim nodded. "Sure, Ma. He's welcome to it. I can sleep on the floor."

Pa Hudson laid the boy carefully on Jim's bed, muttering all the while. "I don't like harboring an Indian in my house. No, sir, I don't." Then he turned to Jim. "You stand guard at the door with Ma's rifle and I'll go back for the melons. Some Indians might come swooping in here to get him."

Ma's eyes flashed as she stooped to pick up her rifle from the floor. "No, Jim. You go help your pa. I'll stand guard."

"All right. We'll be right back," Jim said; he dashed out to join his father.

When they had brought all the melons up to the cabin and stacked them in the shade, they fed and watered the Indian boy's horse. Inside the cabin again they found the boy sound asleep. Now and then, Ma glanced at him as she prepared supper. "Shall we wake him, Pa, and give him something to eat?"

Pa studied the Indian for a few minutes. "No. He's breathing all right but seems in pain. Probably wouldn't want to eat anyway. Let's not bother him."

After supper the Hudsons conversed in low tones. "Where do you suppose he came from, Pa?" Ma asked.

Pa shrugged. "I've no idea, but now we know the Indians have been near our farm."

Ma's blue eyes widened and she shivered slightly. "It makes me fearful, Pa. I've never really been afraid before." She laid a thin, work-worn hand on her husband's brawny one. "Let's go back to Virginia."

Jim glanced quickly at his father and saw Pa's face set in a stubborn mask. He was not surprised to hear his father say, "We can't go all the way back there alone, Ma. It's too dangerous. And there's nothing back in Virginia for us. We were indentured servants, remember. I want to hang on to our farm, all four hundred acres of it."

Ma sighed and smoothed back her faded blond hair.

"But we're free now, Pa. We finished our time of service before we came out here three years ago. And I'd like Jim to have some schooling."

Pa shook his head. "There'd be no future for us in Virginia. We have no money to start back there. Here we have land, our own land. And this is going to be a wonderful country. As for school, you can teach Jim the way you've been doing. Weren't you a governess in one of the big houses of Virginia?"

Jim had been looking from one to the other of his parents, his clear blue eyes sparkling. "Please, Ma," he said, "I want to stay here. You can teach me lots more, and I can help Pa to clear and plant the land."

Pa nodded to Jim and smiled in approval. "There's big men out here, too, from the finest families of Virginia. Men like James Harrod, Robert Todd, Simon Kenton and George Rogers Clark.

"You certainly remember Clark, Ma. His father's land joined where we worked. George Rogers Clark will figure out some way to stop the redskins. You surely don't intend to let one lone Indian boy scare you away from our home."

Ma tried to smile. "No. No Pa, of course not. But we can't be sure there aren't other Indians near at hand."

"That's true," Pa agreed. "You and Jim go to bed. I'll sit up for a while and listen for any unusual sounds."

Ma shook her head. "I'll stay up with you. Jim, I'll make a pallet for you." She got up and fixed a comfortable bed on the floor for Jim. Then she sat down in the cabin doorway beside her husband.

Jim glanced at the Indian boy lying so quietly in his bed, dropped down on the pallet and went to sleep.

Ma and Pa Hudson continued to sit in the doorway, rifles by their side, and to stare out into the silent black night.

When Jim awakened the next morning, Ma had breakfast ready and the Indian boy was looking solemnly at him from his bed.

Jim jumped up. "Good morning, boy," he said with a smile. "What's your name?"

The Indian boy did not reply but kept his brown eyes fixed on Jim.

Ma put a pewter bowl containing steaming hot grits at Jim's place on the table. "Wash your hands and face, son."

"Yes'm." Jim poured some water into the washbasin and began splashing water on his face and hands. As soon as he had finished he carried a pan of water to their strange guest, so he could wash his face.

But the Indian boy just stared at him and did not move.

Ma came over and stood beside the boy. "Come now, boy," she said briskly, "I'll wash your hands and face. Then you must have some breakfast." As she turned one hand over and began to wash it, he tried to sit up, but fell back on the bed with a groan.

"Poor boy. Your shoulder must hurt badly." Ma tried to soothe him as she continued with the washing. "I'll have to get this awful stuff off your face." But when she began scrubbing his face, he groaned again and tried to turn away.

"Maybe it means something to him to wear that vermilion streak," Jim suggested. "Looks like mud, doesn't it? Or it could be he doesn't like water."

Ma wasn't able to get the Indian boy's face thoroughly clean. She brought a bowl of hot grits to him. "Here, boy, try to eat some of this." She held a spoonful of grits to his lips.

The boy tasted it gingerly, found it good and opened his mouth for more. Ma fed him the contents of the bowl while Jim and Pa ate their breakfast.

For several days the Hudsons' strange guest rested in Jim's bed. Now and then he tried to sit up only to lie down again with a low moan. With Ma's good food, however, and excellent care, he did improve and seemed to be less frightened at being with the white family.

Little by little he and Jim began trying to talk to each other. By signs, gestures, and a word or two, each boy began to learn a few words of the other's language.

Jim learned that the Indian boy's name was Wahbunou, which meant The Juggler, and that he had been pulled from his horse when it galloped under a large thorn tree. One of the low branches had brushed him off and a large thorn had pierced his shoulder. He had fallen on a jagged stump and into the tangled wild grapevine, where the Hudsons had found him. But Jim was not able to find out what he was doing near their clearing.

As for Pa, he was disturbed because the Indian boy had been riding so near their farm. Every night after Ma and Jim were asleep, he rose from his bed and sat in the cabin doorway with his rifle ready. But no Indians appeared.

Sometime later Wahbunou was able to be up and about in the cabin. He would watch Pa clean and oil his Deckard rifle, but he never offered to touch it. Soon he began walking around the clearing with Jim and Ma Hudson. He followed Ma everywhere, gratitude for her care shining in his brown eyes.

One morning Pa said, "We'd best have a look at that shoulder, Wahbunou, to see if it's healing properly." But when Pa tried to remove the rag bandage, Wahbunou jerked away like a wounded animal, terror in his eyes.

"Come now, Wahbunou, I just want to look at it," Pa said. "I promise not to hurt you."

But Wahbunou would not permit Pa to touch the bandage.

"Maybe I can show him something new, Pa, and get him calmed down a bit so you can have a look," Jim suggested. "I'll get your drum, Pa. Maybe he's never seen a drum."

Pa shrugged. "Indians have drums, Jim, though not like ours. All right, get it down for him."

Jim climbed on a chair and lifted Pa's drum from its place on the top of Ma's high cupboard. "Look, Wahbunou." Jim took the drumsticks and played a short ruffle on the drum.

Wahbunou seemed interested; he smiled as he reached for one of the sticks. He grasped it gingerly, turning it over and over, finally returning it to Jim who played another ruffle and a loud roll. Wahbunou smiled again and reached for the drum.

Jim nodded. "If you let Pa look at your shoulder, you

may have it." Jim pointed to the Indian boy's shoulder
and then to his father.

Wahbunou drew back, but finally nodded.

Pa took the bandage off, and gently pulled the rough
splint back far enough to look at the boy's shoulder. Then
as gently, he replaced it. "Your wound is healing fine,
Wahbunou. Soon you'll be as good as new."

Jim handed the drum to Wahbunou and the Indian
boy beat out a queer, rhythmical sound with the palm of
his hand. He didn't seem to know how to use the drumsticks. Then the boys took turns beating it. Jim could
make many fancy rolls and ruffles, but Wahbunou could
make only the one sound.

One day was like another at the cabin until nights began to grow much cooler. Pa said any day now there
would be a frost, so they'd soon have to harvest the turnips and corn.

Wahbunou's shoulder healed nicely and Pa finally took
off the bandage and splint. Now that it was cooler and
his shirt was in shreds, Ma said Wahbunou should have a

new outfit of clothes. She had been sewing for Pa and
Jim, so she made Wahbunou a homespun shirt and trousers. In his new clothes Wahbunou looked like any Kentucky boy, save for his copper-colored skin and straight,
coarse black hair.

Not many days after Pa had removed Wahbunou's
bandage, Ma awakened Pa and Jim earlier than usual.
"Jim! Pa!" she cried. "Wake up! He's gone."

"Gone! Who's gone?" Pa asked.

"Wahbunou. He's not in his bed."

Jim had scrambled into his clothes. "He's probably
outside, Ma," he cried as he dashed out-of-doors. But
when Jim looked around their dooryard and in the shed,
he saw that Wahbunou's horse was gone. He ran back
into the house. "Pa, Wahbunou *must* be gone. His horse
isn't in the shed with Nellie, either."

The Hudsons could not believe that Wahbunou would
leave without telling them good-bye; they spent a long
time looking for him. But Wahbunou and his horse were
nowhere in sight.

Finally Ma fixed breakfast. As she put bowls on the table, she sighed and said, "I can't understand why he wanted to leave us. He recovered so nicely and seemed happy here."

Jim looked up from his food. "But Ma, maybe he wanted to go back to his own people. I sure would if I were with the Indians or some other strange folks."

Ma shrugged and brushed her hair back from her forehead. "That was the wrong thing for him to do, Jim ——go away without telling us good-bye. Sneaking off in the night."

Pa looked up at his wife, his brown eyes thoughtful. "Now, Ma, I don't think he did anything so wrong. He was probably afraid we would try to keep him from going, so he just left quietly in the night. I don't believe he was ungrateful. As Jim says, he probably longed for his own people."

Jim finished his breakfast in silence and then suddenly said, "Do you suppose some of the Indians came for him?" Jim's eyes flashed in excitement.

Pa picked up his rifle and put on his homespun jacket. "I don't think they did, Jim, but I'll have a look around to see if there are new tracks of any kind. I believe I would have heard them. He probably just rode off alone."

Ma began to take away the pewter bowls. "I don't like it at all. I feel queer, as if we were surrounded by Indians. I'm afraid we aren't safe here any more."

Chapter II

WAS IT A TRICK?

Not long after Wahbunou's disappearance, a chill north wind blew into the lush Kentucky valley, warning the Hudsons that winter was not far away. Frosty mornings greeted them, and the trees putting on their mantles of brown, red and gold, told them it was time to harvest both turnips and corn.

Jim and Pa spent several days gathering them, while Ma did sentinel duty sitting on a stump with her rifle ready for use. But she was uneasy while on guard, jumping at each snap of a twig.

Finally the corn was shucked and piled high in one corner of the cabin. Pa stored the turnips in a deep hole near the lean-to, so they would keep all winter. One nippy day when the harvest was finished, Pa turned to Jim after breakfast. "Jim, let's go hunting today. I'd like to lay in a supply of game before it gets any colder."

Jim's blue eyes sparkled. "Today, Pa?"

"Today's as good as any time, Jim."

Ma looked troubled. "Must you go, Pa?"

Pa nodded and patted his wife's shoulder awkwardly. "Now Ma, you've been nervous and upset ever since Wahbunou went away. I'd think you'd want us to go hunting. Only yesterday you said you were tired of living on rabbit. You'll be all right here, but don't leave the cabin. We'll be home by early evening."

Ma squared her shoulders and bristled a little. "Pa, I haven't been any more upset than usual. You know I've never liked this country; I want to go back to Virginia." She sighed. "I do know we need fresh meat. Well, I'll spend the day spinning my flax."

Pa's brown eyes sparkled in relief. "That's a good girl, Ma. Who knows? Maybe we'll get a deer. Then you'll have a deerskin to make a jacket and some leggings."

"Or maybe we'll get a bear," Jim boasted.

Soon they were ready to go. Jim was dressed exactly like his father. Each wore home-made moccasins, fur caps, loose thin homespun trousers, topped by long fringed hunting shirts reaching nearly to their knees. Their shirts were held in at the waist by broad belts.

Pa hung his long knife from his belt and Jim started down the clearing, carrying Pa's heavy flintlock rifle. It was as long as Jim was tall and difficult for him to carry, but he tried to manage it proudly.

As Pa went striding through the thick woods, Jim did his best to keep up with him. Now and then a squirrel darted along in front of them, or a few wild turkeys flew over their heads, frightened by their approach.

Jim stopped and started to raise his rifle. "Let's shoot some turkeys, Pa. Ma always likes to cook turkey."

Pa smiled and shook his head. "Not now, Jim. We're

out for bigger game. On the way back we'll bag a few squirrels and turkeys. Then we won't have to carry them so far."

A little farther on, Pa said, "If you should happen to see a bear or deer, Jim, don't be in a hurry to fire. Wait until the animal is close to you. That Deckard works best if you fire it at close range. Always remember, son, don't get excited and fire too soon."

"I'll remember, Pa."

Along about noon Jim suddenly froze in his tracks, certain that he had seen a deer. Pa stopped, glanced in the direction Jim was looking and nodded. The deer evidently had not picked up their scent, as it continued to wander slowly toward them.

Without a sound Jim brought his rifle to rest in a nearby tree notch and waited. When it seemed the approaching deer would surely see them, he fired.

"Good boy, Jim," Pa cried excitedly. "You got him on the first shot."

Jim was elated because it was his very first deer. Of

course he had shot rabbits near their cabin, but a deer was a real triumph. Pa cut a long limb from a tree and stripped off its branches. Then he trussed the deer's legs with a long strip of wild grapevine.

"Now, Jim, help me to run this limb between the deer's legs, so we can carry it easily."

In a jiffy they had the deer slung from the limb. Pa put one end of the limb on Jim's shoulder and the other on his own, so they could carry the animal through the forest without difficulty. It was a fine young buck, and would furnish plenty of meat for them, perhaps even a new hunting shirt.

"Better give me the rifle now, Jim. It's most too heavy for you with that limb on your shoulder. We'll work our way home by Coon Hollow Trace. There's always plenty of game in that neighborhood."

When they arrived at Coon Hollow, a small crossroads in the forest, Jim said, "Look, Pa. I think I see someone coming down that trace." He nodded toward the north.

Instantly Pa laid the deer on the ground and held his

rifle ready. He peered ahead for a moment, then said, "I see two men, Jim, and I think one's leading a pack horse. We'll wait a little."

As the men came nearer, Pa suddenly recognized the taller one. "George Rogers Clark! As I live and breathe." Then he raised his arm in greeting. "Howdy, Mr. Clark. I don't reckon you remember me. I'm Jim Hudson. I used to work the land bordering your father's farm back in Virginia. And this is my son, Jim."

The tall, red-haired man looked at Pa Hudson for a moment and then smiled, his hazel eyes shining and friendly. He shook hands with Jim, then with Pa. "Of course I remember you, Hudson." He gestured toward his companion. "This is Tom Shelton. He's one of the settlers going back to Virginia with me."

"Howdy," Tom Shelton said, shaking Pa's hand.

George Rogers Clark looked inquiringly at the Hudsons. Then he asked, "What are you doing out here so far from Virginia?"

"We came out here three years ago," Pa replied, "to

take up a claim. It's wonderful land; my boy and I are clearing it as fast as we can."

While Pa talked about his dreams for his claim, Jim stared at the splendidly built man his father had called Mr. Clark. He was taller than Pa, young too, and most impressive-looking.

Tom Shelton shook his head when Pa paused for breath. "No more Kentucky for me. I'm beat. I can't take these Indian raids any longer. Last week finished me. My nearest neighbors were attacked and taken prisoners. I got all my possessions with me." He nodded toward the heavily laden pack horse. "Many of us settlers are going back with Colonel Clark. Better join us, Hudson."

"Colonel Clark!" Pa exclaimed. "So you're a colonel now, sir."

The colonel seemed not to have heard Pa's exclamation. He shook his head gravely. "This Indian situation is bad. They're more stirred up than ever this season."

Pa bristled. "There's no Indians going to scare me off

my land. I got a good warm cabin and quite a few acres cleared. I'm staying."

Colonel Clark nodded and smiled. "I like your spirit, Hudson, but if I were you, I'd take my family and crops up to Harrodsburg. Stay there until these Indians quiet down a little."

Pa shook his head. "I mean to stay, sir. I got through last winter all right. We've never been molested."

Colonel Clark put his hand on Pa's shoulder. "We could use more brave men like you out here, Hudson, but the Indians are really on the warpath now. I can't prove it, but I hear Hamilton's paying the Indians for all of the prisoners they deliver to him at Detroit—paying them well, too."

"Hamilton? Who's he, sir?"

"The British commander in charge of all the western country, stationed at Detroit. I hear he's got the Indians really aroused. Better take your family to Harrodsburg for a while."

Pa scratched his ear. "Harrodsburg? That's a far piece

from here. Why not to McClellan's Fort?"

The colonel looked grim. "Haven't you heard, Hudson? Burned out by the Indians early this year."

"Think it over, Hudson," put in Tom Shelton. "Better stay alive in the fort than dead on your claim. Or better yet, go back to Virginia with us. We'll be leaving in a few days, won't we, Colonel?"

Clark nodded. "As soon as I get the settlers together who want to go back with me. I'll be back in the spring."

Pa shifted from one foot to the other. "That's good news, sir, that you'll be back. Thanks for your advice. I'll think it over, but I'm not going back to Virginia. We got to be getting along home now."

The colonel shook hands again with Pa and Jim. "Glad to have seen you, Hudson. Good luck. Better get up to Harrodsburg as soon as you can." He and Shelton moved off along the trace.

When the men had gone and Jim and Pa had been trudging along for a while, Jim asked, "Pa, should we go to Harrodsburg?"

Pa didn't reply for so long Jim was afraid he had made him angry. Finally Pa sighed and said, "I know your ma has been mighty upset since Wahbunou disappeared. And Colonel Clark's not one to be aroused without cause. Maybe we ought to take our meat and provisions to the fort, at least until this Indian scare blows over. I wouldn't want anything to happen to you and Ma."

"But I wouldn't want to lose our farm, Pa."

"We wouldn't lose it, Jim. No Indian's going to squat very long on our land. They're a roving people. The worst they could do would be to burn our cabin, and we could build another one, I guess. But I haven't made up my mind yet, Jim. Better not say anything to your ma about our meeting with Colonel Clark today. No use getting her excited."

"No," Jim agreed. "She's upset enough as it is."

"If I decide we should go," Pa continued, "she'll be glad enough to leave the farm and stay at the fort. So mind now, not a word to Ma."

Jim nodded. "I wouldn't want to worry Ma."

On the way home they shot a squirrel and several wild turkeys, so when they arrived at their cabin, they were well laden with the day's trophies.

"Oh, Pa!" Ma cried, running out to meet them, her blond hair flying. "I thought you'd never come." She clapped her hands when she saw the deer hanging from the limb. "Oh, a deer! Now we'll have plenty of meat."

Pa smiled and pointed toward Jim. "He shot the deer, Ma. Got him on the first shot. We have a squirrel and some turkeys too, so we've a lot of work to do these next few days, jerking this meat."

The next morning was quite cold as a north wind had risen in the valley during the night. But the Hudsons began working early anyway. Jim helped Pa cut the deer meat into long strips and spread it to dry in the sun.

Pa glanced toward the sun. "I think maybe we'll have to smoke this meat after all, Jim. This sun isn't warm enough to cure meat."

Once the norther had passed, however, the weather did warm considerably; Pa said they were feeling the last breath of summer. While father and son worked with the meat, Ma made two new shirts for them and a linsey woolsey dress for herself. She didn't mention Indians again, but she seemed to be uneasy as soon as night fell.

On the evening they had the meat laid by, Pa said casually to his wife, "Ma, I think we'll take our provisions and go up to Harrodsburg for a while."

Jim glanced quickly at his father to see if he had seen or heard anything alarming, but Pa's face showed nothing at all.

Ma gasped in surprise. "To Harrodsburg, Pa? Do you mean to the fort? Why?"

"Well, I've noticed you seem mighty jumpy lately and I thought we'd take our provisions and join the settlers at the fort for a while. It would give you a rest and a chance to hear the news and talk to someone else besides me and Jim. It would be a change."

Ma's face glowed in anticipation and relief. "Oh, Pa, let's do it. Let's go tomorrow before winter sets in and makes us prisoners here."

Pa shook his head. "I'm not sure we can go tomorrow. But we'll start packing."

Ma leaned forward in her chair and searched her husband's face anxiously. "What's made you decide to leave our cabin, Pa? Have you seen signs of Indians?"

Jim looked at his father again as Pa replied almost too casually, "Haven't seen anything, Ma. But we've done the chores and the harvesting, so we can leave the farm for a spell now. Just got a hankering to see people."

Pa's answer seemed to satisfy Ma Hudson because she was up early next morning, and beginning to pack before Jim and Pa were awake. "I'll take my pots and the spinning wheel," she said after breakfast, glancing around their cabin.

Pa shook his head. "You can't take all that stuff, Ma. We've only one horse, remember. We can't put everything we own on Nellie's back. They'll have cooking utensils at the fort and I'm sure some one will have a spinning wheel. We'll take just the corn, turnips and all of our meat."

"May I take your drum, Pa?" put in Jim. "I'll carry it. I can have fun playing it for the other boys at the fort."

Pa hesitated, glancing up at the drum. Then he smiled. "I guess if you want to be responsible for it, you may take the drum. But mind, you hang on to it."

Finally they had the corn packed in two stout cloth sacks and hung on one side of their horse's saddle. Pa put the meat in a peddler's pack which he had brought from Virginia, with most of the turnips on top of the meat. This pack he slung from the other side of the horse's saddle.

Ma had tied a change of clothes and moccasins for each of them in a large square of cloth.

When they were ready to leave, Ma sat on the horse, holding the pack of clothes, while Pa led the horse with one hand and carried his trusty Deckard with the other. Jim walked behind the horse, carrying Ma's rifle, the treasured drum and drumsticks.

As they left their clearing Pa said, "We'll come home as soon as we can."

They trudged along silently, their moccasins and the horse's hoofs, swishing softly through the fallen leaves. Sometimes Ma hummed softly to herself as if she were happy to be on the way to Harrodsburg. But Pa gazed resolutely ahead.

They heard no other sounds for a mile or so.

Then without warning, they found themselves surrounded by a dozen hideously painted Indians. Neither Pa nor Jim could raise their rifles before the Indians had seized and securely bound them.

In trying to raise his rifle, Jim had dropped his drum and sticks, but he was too frightened to notice this.

Ma screamed in terror as one of the Indians leaped upon her horse Nellie, tied Ma's hands and rode off with her into the woods. Two other Indians tied leather thongs around Jim and Pa's waists and began dragging them along behind Ma's captor.

The rest of the band picked up the rifles, drum and sticks and followed along, their whooping and yelling piercing the calm autumn stillness.

Jim was terrified. He wondered if his father were; yet he could do nothing but stumble along behind the Indian who kept jerking the leather thong.

Although Jim was frightened, he did not forget what Pa had said when they found Wahbunou in the woods. Had it been a trick? Were these Indians some of Wahbunou's people? Was this the thanks the Hudsons received for caring for him?

Chapter III

AN EXCHANGE AT THE SALT LICK

The Indians dragged Jim and his father rapidly through the woods until the Hudsons thought they could go no farther. They were happy to reach a small clearing where more Indians were waiting with their women, children and extra horses. To Jim's relief he saw his mother still sitting on their old Nellie.

During her ride, Ma's usually neat blond hair had fallen down over her shoulders. Half a dozen women were crowding around her, fingering her hair and talking excitedly to each other. When they caught sight of Jim's towhead, they laughed and ran their fingers over his hair, too.

Several men were going through the peddler's pack of food. After one look, they dumped the turnips on the ground. But the meat they carefully repacked.

Pa tried to smile reassuringly at Ma and Jim, but one of the men clapped him on the head, picked him up as though he were a feather and dumped him head down across a horse. Then the Indian climbed on behind him. In a moment a second man had done the same to Jim. At once the band rode off with their three white prisoners toward the north.

About dusk they stopped for the night by a small stream. Pulling the Hudsons from their horses, they tied Pa and Jim to one tree, Ma to another. Several women began making fires and filling kettles with water; while other women prepared supper. The children laughed and scampered in and out of the stream. The men paid no attention to their three white prisoners, but sat quietly along the bank of the stream, talking in very low tones.

Jim's head ached so badly from his jolting, upside-down ride through the woods that he could scarcely see. He was glad, though, that his parents were still with him. He looked at the half-grown children playing around the camp, expecting to see Wahbunou, but the boy was not among them.

Ma Hudson was still so frightened she couldn't talk, but she was not so shaken up as Pa or Jim, because she at least had ridden upright.

When supper was ready, one old woman brought scant servings of stew in small gourds to the Hudsons, and three small dry corncakes. Ma wasn't able to eat a bite, but Pa and Jim found the stew surprisingly good. They could have eaten another helping, but the woman did not bring them any more.

After the Indians had eaten their fill, the women banked the fires for the night; men and boys relaxed on the ground. Poor Ma Hudson had either fainted from fright or had fallen into an exhausted sleep.

Pa turned his head slightly toward Jim and whispered, "I'm afraid it was a trick, Jim. Putting Wahbunou with his injured shoulder near our clearing, I mean. He probably reported we could be taken prisoner easily, since we had no near neighbors to help us."

Jim glanced toward the Indian group, then at his father. "But, Pa, Wahbunou isn't with these Indians. All the men and boys are sitting right over there together. Besides, we don't even know if this is Wahbunou's tribe."

Pa looked at the group. Then he nodded his head. "You're right, son. He isn't there."

Jim wriggled a bit trying to loosen the thongs which bound him, but with no success. "I wonder what they'll do with us now, Pa."

Pa tried to shake his dark hair away from his eyes. "Well, since they didn't kill us on the spot, I wonder if they intend to deliver us to Hamilton in Detroit. You remember Colonel Clark said the British commander there was paying the Indians to bring white prisoners to him."

Jim nodded. "Yes, I remember. But why, Pa? And where is this Detroit?"

"You remember when I was in Harrodsburg last year I heard about Great Britain waging a war with our countrymen back east. Now I think this British Hamilton in Detroit is figuring on winning all our Kentucky territory by having the Indians fight for him. They are to scare the settlers into returning back home or to capture them for Hamilton. I'm not sure where Detroit is, but I think it lies far to the north."

Jim glanced toward the Indians again. "Look, Pa. They have our rifles and drum."

Two men were examining the rifles carefully, while the rest of the Indians were passing drum and sticks from hand to hand. One of them began to beat the drum with his hand, making a low rhythmical sound similar to what Wahbunou had made in the Hudson's cabin.

Jim listened intently to the Indians' conversation, but he couldn't understand anything. The words sounded like those Wahbunou had taught him, yet they were somehow different, so that Jim couldn't get even an idea of what was said.

At last they stopped talking and began rolling in their blankets to sleep. Two men came over to the Hudsons, untied Pa and Jim, dragged them to separate trees and secured them again. One Indian rolled in a blanket beside Jim and the other beside Pa. But they offered no blankets to them, nor to Ma Hudson now fifty feet away.

The next morning they gave their prisoners a small amount of food. Ma tasted it and ate a little, but Pa and Jim ate all the Indians gave them. After breakfast, the women packed all the camp equipment together; the men tied the Hudsons' hands, set them upright on horses and scrambled up behind them.

The entire party rode rapidly toward the north and west, arriving late in the afternoon at the broad Ohio River. The men chopped down poplar trees and began building a raft. Jim and Pa Hudson watched in amazement to see how quickly these Indians completed it.

Then they ferried women, children and equipment

across the river. While some Indians guided the raft, others swam their horses to the far side. When all were safely transported, the band set up their camp for the night.

For several days they continued in a northwesterly direction. On a bright cool day they stopped at noon at a salt lick. The Hudsons realized the Indians would stay here for a while, because the women dug a trench, filling it with a great amount of firewood.

When their fires had burned to a bed of red-hot coals, they drew water from the lick and poured it into big salt kettles. These they placed over the hot glowing coals. Some women kept adding firewood to keep the salt water boiling; others began cooking over a second fire.

Pa, Ma and Jim were permitted to walk about the salt lick as far as the long leash around their waists permitted. But the Indians tied them to trees far enough apart so they could not come close to each other. Pa always would smile encouragingly at Ma and Jim, but he was never permitted to touch them. Two Indians were stationed to watch the prisoners, to prevent their escape.

The Indians wanted to build up their supply of salt, so the trench fires under the kettles were not allowed to go out. Several women took turns piling on firewood during the first night.

In the evening one man brought Jim's drum to him, gesturing for him to play it. Jim played his loudest and best, executing ruffles and long rolls for their entertainment. The Indians loved these sounds and his skill with drumsticks, so kept him playing until quite late.

The next afternoon a new group of Indians arrived at the lick; but they kept a long distance away from the trench fires and did not offer to mingle with the first band. They also set up camp and dug a long trench, making a fire and filling their kettles with the brine. This salt lick was evidently common ground, since neither Indian band paid attention to the other.

By nightfall, the women were able to scrape the first salt from the kettles, spread it on rough boards to dry, and to fill the kettles with fresh brine.

Again the men had Jim play his drum for them. Soon

they were swinging their bodies and clapping their hands in time with the drum. Once by the light of campfires, Jim thought he saw shadowy figures creeping close, as if to listen to his playing. He felt uneasy about what they wanted, but he continued to play even louder than before.

In the morning, when the women finally decided they had enough salt for the winter, they began packing their kettles and preparing to leave the salt lick. A few minutes before the band was ready to go, Jim saw four stalwart Indian men advancing rapidly toward them from the other camp. They came near and began making a fire in front of Jim's group.

The men of Jim's camp held a hurried consultation. Then one of them stepped forward, raising his right arm high above his head. Immediately the four visitors came up to him. He motioned for them to be seated; he and his companions sat down, too.

As they talked, Jim thought they must be arguing about some important question. After a long conversation, one visitor rose and walked back to his camp. He soon returned with a white man bound exactly like Pa Hudson.

At a signal from the group sitting on the ground, Jim's guard suddenly untied his leash and led him over to the strangers.

More arguing went on, but the men of Jim's camp kept shaking their heads. Again one visitor returned to his camp, carrying back a handsomely painted buffalo robe which he spread in front of the council. Jim's band examined the robe carefully and nodded their heads. One of them called to the watching men. Immediately an Indian brought Pa Hudson's drum and sticks to the council.

The visitors rose from the ground, handed their white prisoner and the buffalo robe to Jim's band, and motioned to Jim to pick up his drum and sticks. As soon as Jim obeyed, one visitor picked up his leash and led him toward the other camp.

Frightened now, Jim looked back at his parents. Pa was alarmed and Ma, tearful, was holding out her arms toward him, but both of them were still tied to the trees.

When Jim reached the new camp, several men and boys swarmed around him. From their midst, a strangely familiar figure rushed over to Jim and took off his leash.

"Jim! Jim!" he cried. "Don't you remember me? I'm Wahbunou."

Jim dropped his drum in surprise as Wahbunou gave him a friendly thump on the shoulder. "Wahbunou!" he gasped.

Wahbunou was so excited he could scarcely speak, but he had much to tell his friend Jim. "My father and I persuaded Chief Minnemung to trade our white prisoner for you. We couldn't bear to see you remain with the Shawnees. Then we Potawatomis made a fire in front of their camp to show we wanted to counsel with them."

"Shawnees!" Jim cried out in terror, looking back toward his father and mother. The Shawnees, however, were now mounted and moving away from the salt lick. Jim could still see his parents riding on separate horses with their Indian guards, and looking hopelessly toward the Potawatomi camp where Jim had gone.

Jim turned frantically to Wahbunou. "Wahbunou ——my parents! Where are they going? Don't let the Shawnees take them away."

Wahbunou shook his head sadly. "I tried, Jim, I really did. I wanted to have your parents traded to us along with you. But Chief Minnemung was interested only in you and your drum. The drum helped me arrange the trade, too."

"The drum? What do you mean, Wahbunou?"

"The other night," Wahbunou began, "we heard you playing your drum. It was the first time my people, the Potawatomis, had heard such playing. I knew it was not an Indian beating that drum, because I had heard you play like that in your cabin; so I persuaded Chief Minnemung and my father to creep close to the Shawnee camp to listen. It was then I saw you and your parents. I realized you were prisoners of those Shawnees."

"But my parents, Wahbunou. Why aren't they here with me?"

Wahbunou continued patiently. "I asked Chief Minnemung to see if he could get all of you transferred to us. I told him and all our Potawatomi clan how good you were to me when I hurt my shoulder. I pleaded, but Chief Minnemung wanted only you and your drum. Why Jim, he traded his handsomest buffalo robe for your drum."

"But my parents will be unhappy separated from me," Jim persisted.

Wahbunou sighed and nodded. "I know, Jim. But I think no harm will come to them now, because the Shawnees are on their way to Detroit to deliver their prisoners to the great British Hamilton. He pays the Indians well for white prisoners." Wahbunou picked up the drum and sticks. "Come, Jim, I want you to meet my family because soon we will be breaking camp."

Wahbunou's parents, brothers and sisters welcomed Jim heartily into their group. His mother stroked Jim's towhead and said, "Welcome, friend. We Potawatomis will be good to you."

In a short time the Indians began packing to leave the salt lick. When they were ready, Wahbunou said, "Jim, you are to ride with me because we do not have extra horses." He led Jim over to his horse. Jim recognized it as the one he had tied in their lean-to alongside Nellie.

The boys climbed up on the horse. "Now," Wahbunou explained, "we are going to our winter camp. It is still a long distance away. Hang on tight, Jim, because we'll be riding hard today."

Jim did as he was told, but with a heavy heart. Here he was—going to some strange place with Wahbunou and the Potawatomis, while his mother and father were prisoners of the Shawnees. He swallowed hard, wondering if he would ever see them again.

Chapter IV

WINTER WITH THE POTAWATOMIS

The Potawatomis rode hard for several days against a biting northwest wind. Finally they stopped on the banks of the *Au Sable* River, in a wide valley protected by rolling hills. It was an ideal camp site because the hills protected the Indians from bitter winter winds.

Several families had already arrived. Wahbunou told Jim that these people were members of another clan in his tribe. His clan, the Golden Carp, always tried to return to this camp to hear news of their relatives and to share in the tribe's winter sports.

The women began immediately setting up wigwams. These they made with poles fastened to the ground in a circle, and the tops drawn together in a cone. They covered this framework with their *aquapois,* or reed mats made of cattail flags, to shut out snows and winter winds.

The men rested a few days, then decided to go on a short hunting trip to get fresh meat. Early in the morning of the hunt, the men painted their faces with the vermilion, which Jim had first seen on Wahbunou's face.

"Wahbunou," Jim said, "why are the men painting their faces?"

Wahbunou turned from watching his father prepare for the trip. "They always wear it, Jim, when they go hunting or riding for a war raid. The day you found me in your country, I was on a hunting trip with my father and the other men. But I became separated from the rest. I was trying to catch up with them when I was brushed off my horse and broke my shoulder."

"Do you usually hunt near our farm?"

"Oh, no. That was the farthest south and east we had

ever ridden. But hunting wasn't good in the places we knew. If you had not found me I would have died, because my people did not miss me until they returned to camp."

Jim looked puzzled. "But didn't they hunt for you?"

"Oh, yes, for several days. My father said they finally gave me up for lost, thinking I had been killed by a bear."

"Then it wasn't a trick that you happened near our clearing?"

"Trick?" It was Wahbunou's turn to look puzzled. "What do you mean, Jim?"

Jim hesitated. "My father wondered if you had been placed near our farm to spy on us, and see if we could be easily captured."

"Jim! My people would not do that. We have not raided any cabins this year. The prisoner we traded to the Shawnees had fired on Chief Minnemung. We had to capture him. And anyway, Chief Minnemung wanted his knife and gun."

While the boys talked the men finished their preparations and were ready to go. Suddenly Chief Minnemung swung down from his horse and walked toward Jim. "You ride with me today," he said, putting his hand on Jim's shoulder.

Wahbunou gasped in surprise because none of the Indian boys had been asked to go on this hunting trip. Jim looked up at the tall, haughty chief, magnificent in his painted buffalo robe; he started to say he didn't care to go. But the expression on Minnemung's face told him this was not an invitation but a command.

"Yes—yes, sir," he managed, wishing with all his heart he did not have to accompany the chief. "What shall I do to get ready?"

Chief Minnemung looked at him for a moment. "All right as you are. Come." Then he turned and stalked back to his horse.

"It is a great privilege, Jim," Wahbunou whispered, still amazed by the chief's order.

Jim got on the horse behind the chief and the party of eighteen set out for the hunt. After they had ridden a little way into the forest, they separated into groups of two or three going in different directions.

But Chief Minnemung and Jim went alone. As they rode along Jim noticed that the chief was carrying a rifle like his father's, and wearing a long knife also like his father's in a wampum belt which girded his beautiful robe.

Jim pointed to the rifle. "You have a gun like my father's."

Chief Minnemung grinned a hideous grin through his streaked vermilion paint. *"Shemolsea,"* he grunted. Then he patted the big knife and again said, *"Shemolsea."*

Suddenly Chief Minnemung reined in his horse. Then he tried to sight his rifle, but could not do it on the horse, so slid quietly to the ground. Once again he tried to sight the rifle. Jim looked to see what the chief's quarry was. In the distance he saw a black bear, but it was too far away to shoot.

The Indian kept fumbling with the rifle and suddenly the sound of a shot broke the stillness of the forest. Chief

Minnemung shouted in triumph and dropped the gun. He had fired the rifle. But his triumph was short-lived, for his shout was answered by an unearthly moan. He had wounded the bear which was now charging toward him. The old chief stood frozen in his tracks when he realized the rifle shot had not killed the bear.

Jim slid off the horse, grabbed the rifle from the ground, reloaded it and waited. The bear was coming nearer and Jim knew he must not miss his aim. The wounded animal would kill them, if he did not kill it first.

When the bear was only a few feet away, Jim fired. This time the aim was deadly accurate, piercing the bear between the eyes. It fell in its tracks.

Chief Minnemung waited a few moments, then turned to Jim. "White boy, Jim, you have saved Chief Minnemung's life. I will not forget this moment. Minnemung not know how to use *Shemolsea* gun."

The old chief was quite shaken and nervous, but with Jim's help, he managed to truss the bear and get it back

to camp. When the women and children saw Jim and Chief Minnemung returning with the big bear, they ran out to meet them, yelling in delight.

"Bear meat!" Wahbunou cried. "Now we'll have a feast. Chief Minnemung got a bear with *Shemolsea* gun."

The chief was grinning in delight, but never a word did he say about Jim's shooting the bear. He took all the credit for the kill and did not so much as glance at Jim. Jim would have liked to tell Wahbunou he had killed the bear, but he was afraid Chief Minnemung would be angry, so he said nothing.

Late in the day the other men returned with squirrels and wild turkeys, but no large game. For several days the camp feasted on bear meat, while all the Indians praised their chief for bringing home such a prize. The chief still kept silent about Jim.

Soon winter came to the camp and the ground was covered with snow. Then the children had lots of fun. Wah-bunou showed Jim how to make a sled, using buffalo ribs for the runners and hides for the seat. Jim found it was a fine sled and had fun coasting down the hills with the other children.

One morning when the snow was packed very hard, Wahbunou said, "Come on, Jim, we're going to play Snow Snake."

"Snow Snake? What kind of game is that?"

"We play it by teams with snow-snake poles," Wahbunou explained. He took Jim to a long level playground in the valley where the other children had gathered. They chose sides, having six to a team. Then they drew lots to see who would throw the first pole. Wahbunou drew the first throw.

He picked up the hickory pole, the ends of which were carved like the head of a snake. He held it high and threw it with all his strength. The pole shot through the air for quite a distance and fell to the ground far from him. An older boy and girl served as scorekeepers and measured the length of its flight.

"Now, Jim," Wahbunou urged, "do your best."

Jim stepped forward and tried to throw the pole as far as Wahbunou had, but it fell far short. Jim sighed. "I'm no good at this game."

"You'll soon learn, Jim," comforted Wahbunou.

Jim did learn to throw the snow-snake pole as well as the other boys. Sometimes Chief Minnemung walked out to watch the children; he always smiled when Jim threw it farther than the others. Quite often during the winter the chief called Jim to his wigwam, to play Pa Hudson's drum for him and sometimes for all the Indians.

Jim grew tall during the winter, had plenty of food and was snug and warm in the wigwam. He would have been happy with the Potawatomis if only his parents had been with him. But often at night he could not sleep, because he kept seeing his parents riding sadly away with the Shawnees.

After a long, cold winter, spring came again to the valley. One fine day Wahbunou told Jim he had heard the men say they would be moving out of winter camp the next morning.

"But tonight, Jim," Wahbunou went on, "we shall watch the dance of the women. This dance celebrates the beginning of our summer wanderings. Then we'll break up into small bands again and we won't see the rest of our clan until next winter."

Jim looked doubtful. "The dance of the women, Wahbunou? What is that?"

"Wait and see, Jim. Wait and see."

When the women came out of their wigwams in their ceremonial dresses, Jim scarcely recognized any of them. They had greased their hair until it shone in the glow of the campfires, painted their faces with vermilion and put on long white chemises, over which they had strung all the wampum necklaces they possessed.

At their appearance four or five young men began singing and beating the dance rhythm on their Indian drums; often they shook the *si si quoi,* a sort of gourd containing dry seeds. The women danced in graceful rhythm, not missing a single step.

Jim thought the dancing beautiful, but he didn't enjoy

it as much as the Indians, because he grew very sleepy
long before the dance was over. He didn't know it would
last well into the night.

The next morning, however, the camp was awake early
with everyone getting ready to move. The women packed
wigwam poles, cattail mats, kettles, winter buffalo robes
and the rest of the camping equipment. Wahbunou's
mother packed Jim's drum carefully among her belongings, so that he wouldn't have to carry it on the horse.

All the Indians put on their summer clothes, one-piece
garments of red or blue cloth. Wahbunou gave Jim one
of his blue cloth shirts, just like the one he had been wearing when the Hudsons found him. Then everyone
mounted their horses. Once again Jim rode with Wahbunou.

Chief Minnemung started northward with his group.
Jim was to learn they would be constantly on the move
during the spring and summer, as the Potawatomis had
no lands of their own to cultivate. Frenchmen and some
neighboring Indian tribes called them squatters because

of their habit of moving in on land claimed by both the French and Indians.

As they moved back and forth across the Illinois country searching for game, wild berries and edible roots and herbs, spring gave way to summer. Now the prairie grass was as high as Jim's head and the woods dense with foliage.

One morning while Jim was helping Wahbunou's mother skin some squirrels, Wahbunou wandered away on some mission of his own. Wahbunou didn't like to work; he specially didn't want to skin squirrels, so he always managed to get away when his mother needed him. He was gone only a few minutes, however, then came rushing back. "Jim. Jim, Chief Minnemung wants to see you at once."

Jim put down a squirrel and looked up. "Chief Minnemung? Where is he? I wonder what he wants."

Wahbunou pointed to a group of men under a tree. "He's over there. See? Talking with my father and some of the other men."

Jim turned to Wahbunou's mother. "I'll be back soon. Chief Minnemung wants to speak to me." Then he walked over toward the group of men.

At his approach the men nodded and walked away from their chief. Minnemung smiled at Jim and motioned for him to sit down beside him.

"Jim," he said, laying his hand on the boy's arm, "I have been watching you all winter and spring. Now I have come to a great decision."

Jim waited, wondering what the old man would say next.

Chief Minnemung leaned toward the boy, his brown eyes stern and serious. "I have decided to adopt you as my own son."

"Adopt me!" Jim gasped, a chill of fear passing over him.

The old chief continued as though Jim had not spoken. "I lost my only son two years ago with a fever. That fever took four of our most promising young men. I have been lonely, very lonely in my wigwam. But I have watched you all during the time you have been with us. I remember also that you saved my life on that hunting trip when I did not know how to use the rifle of the *Shemolsea.*"

Chief Minnemung did not take his eyes from the trembling boy. "But the greatest test of all you passed easily. You did not belittle me in front of my clan by telling them that you killed the black bear."

Jim was startled. He hadn't realized that Minnemung would have lost the esteem of his clan if the Indians discovered Jim had really killed the bear.

"So you see," Chief Minnemung continued, "you have proved yourself worthy of adoption into the Potawatomi tribe as my son."

"Adoption," Jim murmured. It was the last gift he wanted, because it would mean he would be forever cut off from his own people. "But sir—" he began.

"We shall have the adoption ceremonies when the clans gather early in the fall," the chief said. "I just wanted to tell you of this honor which awaits you." Chief Minnemung nodded his head in dismissal. "That is all."

Jim stumbled back; Wahbunou and his mother were still working with the squirrel skins.

"What's the matter, Jim?" Wahbunou asked, when he caught sight of Jim's stricken face. "Was Chief Minnemung angry with you? And for what?"

Jim shook his head. "No, he wasn't angry. He wanted to tell me that he is going to adopt me as his son in the fall."

Wahbunou dropped the skin he was cleaning. "Chief Minnemung is going to adopt you!" Wahbunou clapped Jim on the back. "Why, that means you'll be the son of a chief."

Jim hung his head and said in a low voice, "Wahbunou, I don't want to be adopted by Chief Minnemung. And I don't want to be a member of your tribe."

Wahbunou stared at Jim, thinking he had not heard him correctly. "You don't want to be Chief Minnemung's son?"

Now Jim's blue eyes were misty with tears. "No, Wahbunou. You and your people have been very kind to me, but I want my own people. I hope to find my father and mother. Don't you remember that you didn't want to live with us?"

Wahbunou nodded slowly. "But, Jim, you don't know where your father and mother are. Nor do I. I only know they were prisoners of the Shawnees. And they live far to the east. We Potawatomis do not mingle with them."

Jim's lips trembled as he said, "If they're still alive, I'll find them some day, Wahbunou. I wouldn't be happy being a real Potawatomi."

Wahbunou sighed and was silent for a while. Finally he said, "Jim, I do understand that you want to be with your own people. Believe me. But Chief Minnemung has spoken. His word is law with us. There is nothing that my father or I can do to prevent your adoption."

Chapter V

THE LONG-KNIVES

Several days later Chief Minnemung sent word around that everyone was to prepare for the annual trading trip to Cahokia. Soon the women were busy sorting the fur pelts they had accumulated during the winter and spring, and tying them in separate bundles according to kind. When all were sorted, Jim was surprised to see how many bundles there were.

"This Cahokia, Wahbunou? What is it?" Jim asked. He and Wahbunou were mounted on the horse ready to start on the journey.

Wahbunou smiled. "Cahokia is a French village a long way from here. We go there every year about this time. The French have a trading post and we'll trade our furs for many supplies which we need."

"What supplies, Wahbunou?"

"I'm not sure what we'll get this trip, but sometimes we get food or blankets. I think Chief Minnemung may want to trade for guns and some powder. The French are our friends; we always stay a while in their village. Then we'll move on for the annual council of our tribe."

A shadow crossed Jim's face at mention of the council, because Minnemung had told him the adoption ceremonies would take place there. Suddenly a plan of escape from the Potawatomis occurred to him. Perhaps he might be able to join the French while trading was going on; they might even help him find his parents. But he said nothing to Wahbunou.

The Potawatomis had been wandering southeast, but now they turned about and began riding in a westerly direction, bearing a little to the north. It was so warm they didn't try to cover many miles in a day. Sometimes they stayed several days in their overnight camps. This was the season for ripe berries, so the Indians stopped often to feast on wild raspberries or dewberries.

One afternoon they happened upon a large berry patch bordering a heavy forest. Everyone ate his fill of berries while the women and children gathered some in their kettles and gourds to take with them. Wahbunou told Jim they would be leaving the forests now and riding through wide meadows of prairie grass. There would not be another opportunity to pick berries this summer.

The two boys tethered their horse, scrambling farther and farther into the brambles away from the rest of the Indians and seeking larger and larger berries. All at once Jim looked back and saw the Potawatomis riding away without them.

"Wahbunou!" he cried. "Look! Minnemung and the rest are leaving."

Wahbunou glanced toward the disappearing group. "In a minute, Jim. We can catch them easily. Let's get just a few more berries." He pointed to a heavily laden bush nearby. "Let's get those, then we'll go."

Jim glanced uneasily at the band of Indians now almost out of sight in the tall prairie grass. He didn't want to be left in this trackless ocean of grass. "We'd better go, Wahbunou."

Wahbunou tossed his head and laughed. "I can catch them easily, Jim. My horse isn't far away and he's faster than any save Chief Minnemung's." Then he turned again to the berries. The boys had been stuffing themselves with the delicious fruit for perhaps ten minutes, when Wahbunou's horse suddenly began pawing the ground. Wahbunou cocked his head to one side and listened.

"I hear the sound of many feet, Jim. I think it's the feet of many men." Now it was Wahbunou's turn to be alarmed.

Jim frowned. "I don't hear anything, Wahbunou. Let's be on our way."

"You wait," cautioned Wahbunou, seizing his horse's

bridle. "I don't hear any horses' hoofs, just the sound of men." He led his horse to the edge of the berry patch, where he could see the broad expanse of prairie. The grass was almost as tall as Jim's head, it rippled rhythmically in the wind, making it look like waves of the ocean. It had a sort of singing sound which Jim had never heard before.

"I hear only a sort of singing," Jim said. "I think it's the wind in this grass."

Wahbunou put his finger to his lips. "Shh, Jim! They're coming." Then he signaled to his horse to lie down at the edge of the grass.

The horse obeyed immediately and none too soon either. The next moment the boys saw a band of white men marching out of the forest. And they kept coming, more men than Wahbunou could count. Just before they plunged into the thick prairie grass the boys could see they had long rifles and wore sparkling long knives in their belts. The sun shining on the knives made them visible even at this distance.

"*Shemolsea!*" gasped Wahbunou, dropping to his knees.

Jim also dropped down into the grass and turned to Wahbunou. "Wahbunou," he whispered, "what do you mean by *Shemolsea?* I remember you said that word the day my father found you in the woods. And Chief Minnemung said his rifle was *Shemolsea.*"

Wahbunou whispered, "*Shemolsea*—Long-Knife. Men who carry long knives. You know your father had one. He is *Shemolsea.*"

"Oh! You mean all of us Kentucky settlers are Long-Knives?" Jim started to stand up, but Wahbunou pulled him down. "Do you want them to kill you, Jim?" he whispered in terror.

"Why, they wouldn't kill us. Maybe I might know some of them." Jim raised up to take another look at the men. Their column had turned southwest and Jim could no longer see their faces. There were so many men Jim was afraid to call out to them. "I wonder who they are and where they're going," he muttered, half to himself.

Wahbunou was whispering, "As soon as they've gone, we'll have to ride fast and tell Chief Minnemung about the many, many Long-Knives we've seen."

"I think I'll go and join them," Jim cried, scrambling up from the tall grass.

Wahbunou tripped him and he fell headlong. "No, Jim. That you cannot do. Chief Minnemung would kill me if anything happened to you. You must ride back with me."

Wahbunou looked so frightened that Jim hesitated. He wouldn't want Wahbunou punished by Chief Minnemung; nor would he want those Long-Knives, whoever they were, to attack the little Potawatomi band. For a few minutes he was silent. Then he said, "Wahbunou, I'll go back with you, if you'll promise not to tell anyone we saw these Long-Knives. Promise?"

"But maybe they'll attack us," Wahbunou replied doubtfully.

"Aw, those men aren't marching after a small band of Indians," Jim replied. "Is there any town near here?"

"Kaskaskia is over that way." Wahbunou pointed in the general direction the column of men had taken. "It's another French settlement. We do not go through it on the way to Cahokia. Cahokia is north."

Jim shook his head. He still wondered where those Long-Knives were going—his Long-Knives. Why, they were his people! Suddenly he thought of another plan of escape, this time without involving Wahbunou. Here was his real chance. He turned to tell the Indian boy, but Wahbunou was on his feet signaling to his horse.

"Come, Jim. The Long-Knives have gone. I think we can ride now." Wahbunou mounted his horse and Jim climbed on behind him.

As they rode through the prairie grass away from the column of Long-Knives, Jim said, "Wahbunou, I can't go through with it. I can't let Chief Minnemung adopt me into the Potawatomi tribe. My countrymen are close at hand. I can join these white Long-Knives and perhaps they will know something of my father and mother."

Wahbunou trembled as he cried out, "Jim! You must

not leave me. You must go back to Chief Minnemung. He will kill me if I return without you."

Jim became thoughtful; then he said, "Wahbunou, it wouldn't be your fault if I left the camp tonight."

Wahbunou gulped. "You wouldn't dare do that, Jim."

Jim nodded. "Wouldn't I? You did. You stole away from us and went back to your people."

The Indian boy urged his horse to a faster pace. "Yes, Jim, I did. My people were going to a place I knew and I had a horse. You wouldn't take my horse?"

"No, Wahbunou, I wouldn't steal your horse. But you must promise not to tell anyone about seeing the Long-Knives. I'll steal away at night. I'll find those men."

"But, Jim, you'd get lost in the dark. And Chief Minnemung would hear you. Indians have sharp ears."

"I'll have the stars to guide me. My father taught me to tell direction by the stars. The Long-Knives certainly won't march all night. I'll find them, never fear." Jim clutched Wahbunou more firmly. "Now promise me— no word about the Long-Knives."

Wahbunou gulped and finally said, "It shall be as you say. Wahbunou will say no word."

Thus the two boys made a solemn pact riding back to the Potawatomi band.

When they finally arrived, the Indians had pitched camp in a small thicket adjoining the prairie. It was almost dark and the women had supper ready. Strangely enough no one had missed them, so the boys didn't have to explain their absence. Evidently the Indians had neither heard nor seen the marching column of men, because they seemed as carefree as usual.

After supper, as the Indians sat around the campfire, Chief Minnemung suddenly took a notion to have Jim play his drum. "Jim," he said, "get your drum and play for us."

Nothing could have pleased Jim more. If his Long-Knives were within hearing distance and heard the roll of the drum, they might investigate the sound. He didn't want to see his Indian friends hurt, but he did wish the Long-Knives would appear and take him with them. He rose quickly. "Yes, Chief Minnemung, I'll be glad to play for you."

Wahbunou's mother had to unpack the drum from her housekeeping belongings, but she did not protest because Chief Minnemung had ordered Jim to play.

Jim beat the drum with all his might, executing some long rolls and difficult ruffles. Now and then he would toss a drumstick into the air and catch it again without missing a beat. At this the Indians grinned in glee at his skill.

Jim played until he was exhausted, all the while hoping to see the Long-Knives coming to the camp. But no one came, and nothing broke the stillness of the summer night save the beating of his drum.

At last Chief Minnemung signaled for him to stop playing. Immediately all the Indians lay down to sleep. Wahbunou's mother forgot to pack Jim's drum away, so he put it carefully down on the ground between him and Wahbunou. Then he lay down and pretended to sleep.

He listened for a long time until he felt sure everyone

was asleep; then he took his drum and began to crawl slowly from his place on the ground. But Wahbunou was not asleep. At Jim's first move he whispered, "Jim, are you leaving?"

Jim turned and patted Wahbunou's shoulder. "Shh! Yes. Thanks, Wahbunou. I'll never forget you."

Wahbunou sighed but did not reply, so Jim felt sure his secret was safe with his Indian friend. Wahbunou would not fail him.

He continued to inch along the ground with the drum, stopping every few feet to see if any of the other Indians had awakened; but save for Wahbunou, the camp was silent.

When he was certain he was far enough away not to be seen, Jim stood up; he fastened his drum and drumsticks to the belt encircling his long blue shirt, and looked at the sky. It was a beautiful summer night and the sky was filled with stars.

He studied them for a few minutes until he located the North Star and the Big Dipper. Then he began walking southwest, the way the Long-Knives had marched in the afternoon. Except for twinkling stars, the night was very black, because there was no moon.

Jim trudged along and was soon beyond the little thicket, which broke the vast prairie. All through the long night, he made his way through the high prairie grass, hearing no sound save the singing of the wind.

When morning finally came, he found himself in the midst of a trackless ocean of grass, with no sign of any Long-Knives, no telltale path through the grass or sign of the Indians' camp. There was only singing, swaying prairie grass, stretching toward the horizon in all directions.

Jim sighed, but walked steadily on, now and then scaring up a flock of prairie chickens which rose squawking into the air. Taking his bearings from the sun now, he knew he was going west.

The sun grew unbearably hot, making Jim very thirsty, but there was no water anywhere. Now and then he would look back to see if the Indians could be pursuing him. But he needn't have worried. His slight figure left no trail through the prairie grass.

As the day wore on he became thirstier, and very hungry. He began to wonder if he had made a mistake to leave the Indians and try to find a band of strange men in this trackless country. Late in the afternoon he thought he saw a line of trees in the distance. He couldn't be sure, because this steaming prairie grass played tricks with his eyes and he was afraid he saw a mirage. If he could only make it to those trees, he would lie down in the shade and rest a bit.

The trees proved to be real enough, and when Jim reached them he fell into their cool shade and feel asleep.

He was awakened after dawn by someone prodding his foot and a rough voice saying, "Get up, boy. Who are you? Where did you come from?"

Jim opened his eyes and saw two men standing over him. They were dressed in dirty, torn buckskins, with long knives hanging to their belts. The taller man was prodding him with a rifle.

Jim sprang up, his eyes shining. "Oh, you're the *Shemolsea*—the Long-Knives."

"Never mind who we are," the man said crossly. "Who are you in that Indian outfit? What are you doing here?"

"I'm Jim Hudson. I escaped from the Indians last night and I've been trying to find you all day."

"A likely story," muttered the shorter man. "Probably you're some spy sent out by the Indians."

Jim shook his head. "No, sir. I saw a big band of Long-Knives yesterday and I've been trying to find them."

"Let's take him to Colonel Clark," the shorter man suggested.

Jim's eyes sparkled. "Clark, did you say? George Rogers Clark? Is he red-haired?"

The tall soldier spoke again. "Say, boy, you know too much. Come on, get going."

As they walked single file through the woods, they made Jim walk between them. After stumbling over fallen trees and brambles for about a mile, they came upon a group of ragged men sitting and standing in the dense shade along a river.

"Colonel Clark, sir," began the tall soldier, "we've found a white boy; he says he was a prisoner of the Indians. But he knows too much. Must be some trick here."

A ragged, commanding figure with red hair turned from the men and walked over to Jim. His stern, hazel eyes seemed to penetrate Jim's whole body as he said, "Well, lad, who are you? What are you doing here?"

Jim was so excited he could scarcely talk. "Colonel Clark, I'm Jim Hudson. I don't suppose you remember me, sir, but I remember your red hair. I met you late last year with my father at Coon Hollow. We had been hunting and had bagged a deer. You advised my father to go to Harrodsburg until the Indian scare was over." Jim looked hopefully at the colonel.

Colonel Clark seemed to be turning something over in his mind. Finally he smiled. "I remember. But how do you happen to be out here in the Illinois country?"

Then Jim told the long story of how he and Pa and Ma had been captured by the Shawnees on the way to Harrodsburg; how later he had been traded to the Potawatomis, with whom he had spent the winter. When he was telling of seeing the column of Long-Knives, Colonel Clark interrupted him.

"Just a minute, boy. Did the Indians with you see us?"

Jim shook his head. "No, sir, only Wahbunou. We had stayed behind the rest to eat more berries. Wahbunou promised me he would not tell he had seen the Long-Knives."

Colonel Clark looked puzzled. "That's hard to believe, Jim. I wouldn't trust an Indian not to warn his people of an army of white men near them."

The tall soldier scowled, as did several others. But no one spoke a word.

"But, sir," Jim replied, "we saved Wahbunou's life, so he promised not to tell about the Long-Knives. He knew of my plan to escape." Jim explained how the Hudsons found Wahbunou near their clearing and of Chief Minnemung's decision to adopt Jim. "That's why I ran away, sir. I didn't want to be a Potawatomi. I hope to find my parents, but I don't know if they're alive."

George Rogers Clark nodded. "I trust they are, Jim, and I can't blame you for not wanting to be a Potawatomi. For the present you'll go with us and be a part of my volunteer army. We're crossing the river tonight and marching on Kaskaskia."

"I see you have a drum. Perhaps we'll need a drummer before this night is over." He turned and motioned to the tall soldier. "This is Simon Kenton, Jim. You are to go with him and do whatever he says."

"Yes, sir."

Simon Kenton inclined his head toward the river bank. "Come on, Jim. We'll have a look at Kaskaskia from this side of the river. Have a care though. We don't want any of those Frenchmen over there to see us."

As Jim and Kenton approached the river's edge, Kenton dropped to the ground. "We have to crawl now, Jim, so's we can see without being seen."

At the edge of the bank they could see the little town of Kaskaskia. It lay in a kind of amphitheatre of woods and bluffs. They could also see the fort with a stockade built around it, the steeple of a church, and some thatched roofs and stone houses shining in the afternoon sun.

"Gee, it's bigger than the settlements I've seen in Virginia!" Jim exclaimed.

"Yep," Kenton replied. "This is one of the oldest and best of the French villages. I've heard it called the Paris of the West. See that British flag flying above the fort? Tomorrow, God willing, it'll be flying the American flag.

"You see, Jim, Colonel Clark has to take this country from the British to make our Kentucky settlers safe from Indian attack. Commander Hamilton at Detroit has been stirring up the Indians against our people."

"Yes, sir, I know. I think that's how my parents and I happened to be captured."

For a while they watched the town. Nothing unusual was going on, so Simon Kenton told Jim he thought no one there suspected the presence of Clark and his army directly across the river. Then they crawled back to the main group of soldiers.

Jim didn't think the men in this motley, exhausted army could capture a town during the night. Several of them had taken off their shoes and were nursing their painful, swollen feet. They were suffering from scald foot, a wilderness malady brought on by dampness, heat and too much marching.

Jim wondered if they could put on their shoes when it came time to cross the river. All of them were hungry besides, as they had eaten nothing but berries for many days. Could such an army capture a well-fed town like Kaskaskia?

Chapter VI

ON TO KASKASKIA

When night fell, Colonel Clark ordered his men to march. Led by two soldiers who had been scouting the woods all afternoon, they followed the bank of the Kaskaskia River until they came to a farmhouse. Here several boats were moored at the river bank. Clark ordered some of his men to surround the house and others to seize the family living in it.

A very frightened Frenchman, his wife and their several children came out of the house, holding their hands high in the air. The soldiers brought the father to Colonel Clark who began questioning him about the town of Kaskaskia.

The man said the town had been expecting an attack from the direction of the Mississippi River. This alarm had died down, he thought, because now there was no extra militia at Kaskaskia. He also said most of the Indians loitering there had left and gone to Cahokia.

Jim shivered at the mention of Cahokia and wondered if Chief Minnemung and his Potawatomis had arrived there, or if they were still searching for him.

When Clark got the information that the town was quiet, he permitted the French family to return to their home, and ordered his men to start ferrying the army across the river. Since he had well over a hundred men, they must make many trips back and forth in the few boats on the river bank. Jim and Simon Kenton were to go with the first group.

As Jim climbed into one boat, he stumbled over a boy about his own age who was trembling and cowering in the bottom. Kenton, just behind Jim, pointed his rifle at the boy. "Who are you?" he asked gruffly. "What are you doing here?"

The frightened boy did not reply but stared up at the rifle.

"Come, boy," Kenton repeated, "what are you doing here?"

The boy scrambled to his feet and stammered, "I—— I was just going home. I came from Kaskaskia this morning in this boat. I was hunting beeswax for Father Gibault. He needs more beeswax for the church candles. When I saw all your men I hid here. I hoped you would go away so I could go home."

Kenton sneered. "A likely story. You've been spying for de Rochblave no doubt."

"Oh, no, sir. I only know the commandant by sight, sir. I tell you true, I was hunting beeswax. And I found a bee tree, too."

"Well, you'll go back as our prisoner. Sit down in the boat." Simon Kenton turned to Jim. "Sit beside him,

Jim, and keep your eye on him. Don't let him get away."

"Yes, sir," Jim replied, making room for the boy.

The boat was now filled and the men began rowing across the river toward Kaskaskia. Jim could feel the boy trembling beside him. He whispered, "Don't be afraid. Colonel Clark will see that no harm comes to you. What's your name? I'm Jim Hudson."

"Willie—— Willie Watson," the boy replied.

As soon as all soldiers were ferried across the river and assembled in their respective companies, Colonel Clark stepped out in front of them. It was too dark to see this erect, commanding man, but there was no mistaking the stern authority in his voice.

"Men," he said, "our first objective is to take this town. By seizing Kaskaskia, we'll be protecting our countrymen in the western country. You all know the British have been inciting the Indians to war against our settlers. By controlling this French settlement, we'll cut off all supplies from New Orleans and the west to Hamilton at Detroit, so tonight it's win or lose everything. Now,

I'll make three divisions of these companies. Captain Bowman."

"Yes, sir," and Captain Bowman stepped forward.

"You are to command one division. Take your men to the far quarter of the town. Captain Helm, command the second, and take your men to the other end of town. I'll lead the third division."

The men assembled quickly according to orders. Jim and Willie were assigned to Captain Bowman's division.

"Kenton," Colonel Clark continued, "you're to go with me. Now, men, if we take the fort and capture de Rochblave without resistance, you'll hear three shots. The shots will be my signal of victory. Then all of you are to yell and shout as loudly as you can. And Jim," Colonel Clark peered into the darkness, "where's Jim Hudson?"

"Here, sir."

"When the men start yelling, you beat your drum as hard as possible. Run through the town from one end to the other beating it. That will help make the French think we have a large army. Keep beating it. Do you hear?"

"Yes, sir."

"If any of you men speak French, step forward."

Several soldiers stepped forward from the ranks.

Willie whispered to Jim, "I can speak French, too."

"Step forward then," Jim urged, so Willie stepped out with the others.

"After I give the signal," Clark continued, "you are to run through the streets telling the people in French that the Long-Knives have taken Kaskaskia. And tell them to stay inside their homes. If they venture outside they will be shot." Clark's voice became sterner than before. "Now then, not one of you is to talk to any of the inhabitants. I want no conversation with them. Is that clear?"

"Yes, sir," the men answered in chorus.

Immediately Colonel Clark set out, leading his own division through dark, silent streets toward the fort. The

two captains started with their men for the assigned po-
sitions. For Jim and Willie it was an eerie experience to
march through the dark streets, then wait—wait in silence
for the hoped-for signal.

After what seemed an endless time to the boys, three
rifle shots rang out from the fort. These meant that
Colonel Clark and his men had captured Commandant
Philip de Rochblave and his fort without any resistance.

Then what yelling and screaming went up in all parts
of the town. Those men speaking French tried to out-
yell other Long-Knives shouting Clark's orders in English. As Willie ran through the streets shouting his orders, Jim kept beside him, beating his drum with all his
might.

Jim thought he'd better keep track of Willie so he
wouldn't escape. Willie, however, showed no signs of
wanting to leave the Long-Knives, but kept shouting
Clark's orders over and over. They kept up this din all
night and were so excited they never thought of sleep.

The next morning the streets were deserted save for

Clark's troops now doing guard duty in various parts of town. Jim and Willie were still together and Jim was surprised to see what a beautiful place Kaskaskia was.

In the center of town was a large grass-covered square, with narrow streets leading out from it. From here Jim saw the American flag was indeed flying from the old fort. There were a few stone houses here and there, but most of them were wooden with pointed, thatched roofs and chimneys at either end.

While Jim was admiring the town, someone called, "Come on, boys. Breakfast is ready."

Jim and Willie didn't need to be called the second time. They dashed to join the men just sitting down to breakfast; it had been prepared by spies Colonel Clark had sent into town ahead of his troops.

Meantime the terror-stricken residents of Kaskaskia remained indoors, not knowing what was to become of them. Father Pierre Gibault asked Colonel Clark if the people could assemble in the church to pray. They feared they were to be separated and taken away by Clark's soldiers. Clark granted Father Gibault's request and the people walked solemnly into the church.

Some time later Colonel Clark spoke to them, telling them not to be afraid. He said the king of France had joined the Americans against the British and now they could all work together. He asked only that the residents of Kaskaskia swear allegiance to the Long-Knives, who represented the Continental Congress and Virginia.

Immediately the gloom and fear of the people melted away. They rang the old church bell in jubilation, giving thanks for their freedom, weeping and laughing for joy.

No one was more astounded at this news than little Willie Watson. He clapped his hands and turned handsprings down the street. He had expected to be thrown into chains and taken far away. Now he was as free as Jim. He looked at his friend. "Colonel Clark is a wonderful man," he said, his dark eyes shining.

Jim nodded. "Willie, were you really hunting beeswax across the river?"

"Of course I was, Jim. We have no wax for the church

candles, so I went to hunt a bee tree. Now I'll get some-one to go with me to get the honey and wax."

"Are you responsible for the candles, Willie?"

"Not entirely, Jim. I am a ward of Father Gibault and I help him in any way I can.

"My father was a river man on the Ohio. He worked for Boynton, Wharton and Morgan Company. They used to send boatloads of merchandise from Philadelphia down the Ohio and up the Mississippi Rivers to their store here. My father made many trips for them, but he was drowned in 1772. So Father Gibault found a house for my mother and me next door to him."

"Then you live with your mother?"

"Yes, I do. She sews for some of the wealthy people and mends for Father Gibault. In the winter I work for Monsieur Gabriel Cerré."

Jim's face was sad for a moment. "My mother was a good seamstress, too."

Willie was puzzled. "Say, where are your mother and father? How do you happen to be with Clark's army?"

Then Jim told Willie about the last time he had seen his parents and what had happened to him since.

"That's too bad, Jim," Willie said. "Of course Indians do sometimes kill their prisoners, but it's likely your parents are still alive. What are you going to do now?"

Jim sighed. "I hope I'll find them some day. Maybe Colonel Clark will have a job for me. I'd like to stay with him and his men."

Willie smiled. "If he doesn't, Jim, I think I can get you a job working with me. Monsieur Cerré is a big merchant here and needs quite a few people in the fall. He's away from Kaskaskia right now."

Jim nodded. "I may ask you later, Willie, because I have to find something to do."

"Guess I'd better go home now, Jim. Will you come home with me?"

"No thanks, Willie. I have to see what Colonel Clark has in mind for me."

"Well, good-bye, for now," and Willie ran happily down the street toward Father Gibault's house.

Jim walked slowly over to Colonel Clark's headquarters. When he arrived Captain Bowman and a few French citizens were just leaving. Clark was giving them last-minute instructions.

"Captain Bowman," he was saying, "use all your persuasive powers and those of these good citizens," he nodded toward the Frenchmen, "to get the people of Cahokia to swear allegiance to our Continental Congress. No violence, though."

"Yes, sir," Captain Bowman replied, saluting smartly. "I think I can win them over with the help of these men." Then he and the Frenchmen left headquarters for their ride to Cahokia.

After they had gone Colonel Clark noticed Jim standing in the room. "Hello, Jim. What is it?"

"I wonder, sir," he began, "if you have a job for me. You see I have no home here, as Willie has."

Colonel Clark frowned for a moment and then smiled. "To be sure, I have a job for you, Jim. You can be my personal messenger. Now that we have won Kaskaskia,

I have to deal with the Indian tribes camped in this neighborhood."

"Yes, sir."

"Are you a good penman, Jim?"

"I can write a good hand, sir. My mother used to be a governess in Virginia and she taught me to read, write and figure."

"Good. I have a lot of letters to write and you can help me with them, too. You'll sleep here at headquarters and eat with my men. Tomorrow you'll have plenty of work to do."

"Oh, thank you, sir." Jim's heart was singing. All would be well with him if he could stay with Colonel Clark.

Chapter VII

NO ADOPTION

George Rogers Clark's sudden appearance in the French settlements with his army threw the Indians camping there into a panic. They thought the army larger than it was and expected to be attacked momentarily. Some tribes asked their French friends in Kaskaskia and Cahokia what they should do.

The French, who were now firm friends of the Long-Knives, advised them to call upon Clark and sue for peace. Then these same Frenchmen reported to Clark that the Indians had come to them for advice.

Colonel Clark was quick to take advantage of the Indians' confusion. He prepared a letter to be sent to the tribes, telling them to lay down their tomahawks and ally themselves with him, or to fight like men for the English. Jim Hudson made several copies of this letter, which Clark sent by him and other messengers to the different tribes.

The Kickapoos and Piankeshaws signed treaties immediately with the Long-Knives. Other tribes, however ——the Chippewas, Ottawas, Potawatomis, Sacs and Foxes——came into Cahokia and demanded a council with Clark. They wanted to see the chief Long-Knife and to hear what he had to say.

Colonel Clark sent word to them that he would attend their council, but he took his time about going to Cahokia to meet with them. He thought it would be well for the Indians to wait on him. After a while he took Jim Hudson, some of his officers and many of his soldiers to Cahokia, which had sworn allegiance to him through Captain Bowman.

Clark's new headquarters were in a house beside the Cahokia River. In a few days a band of Winnebagos, often called Stinkers by the French, pitched camp in a Frenchman's yard, just across the road from Clark's headquarters.

When Jim Hudson saw the Indians he was frightened and said to Colonel Clark, "I don't think those Stinkers should camp so near you, sir. They might attack us. We don't have many soldiers here."

The colonel's eyes twinkled. "How right you are, Jim. I think they have something like that in mind. Perhaps they want to kidnap me so I can't appear at the council."

Jim shivered. "Oh, sir! Can't you recall some of the men you have stationed around the town?"

"Jim, you have the mark of a military man," Colonel Clark replied. "That's what I intend to do, but I don't want these Stinkers to know about my reinforcements. You go to my captains now and tell them to send several guard details to my headquarters as soon as it is dark. Tell them to come in one by one at the rear."

"Yes, sir," Jim replied, glad to have an errand and to know they were to have more soldiers at headquarters. He dashed out to find Captain Helm and Simon Kenton.

That evening fifty guards began filtering into headquarters, some to conceal themselves in the house, others to stand in the darkness outside. Although Clark walked alone about the yard, nothing happened.

The next night the guards again took up their same stations. Colonel Clark stayed up late, supposedly working on reports.

Jim couldn't sleep, so he went to the window and stared out into the night. About one o'clock shots were fired across the river. In a few minutes Jim saw some skulking figures in the headquarters yard. He wanted to scream, but Clark himself gave the alarm.

Immediately the guards appeared from all sides of the building. They succeeded in capturing three of the Stinkers and hustled them into headquarters. The shots and ensuing racket awakened the town; some of the citizens hurried to headquarters to see what was the matter.

To Jim's great surprise, the colonel asked these French-men what punishment they thought these Stinkers de-served. In one voice they said these Indians should be put in irons. Then and there, Clark made this an order. Thus he maneuvered so that the French suggested the punishment for the Indians.

The next morning Colonel Clark went to the great In-dian council, accompanied by some of his officers and townsmen. At the last minute he told Jim he might go. He also had the three Stinkers brought to the council in chains. How ridiculous they looked clanking along be-side the officers.

Jim was amazed at the number of Indians awaiting Colonel Clark's arrival. Jim looked over the crowd to see if he could see Chief Minnemung or any of his Potawat-omis. If they were there he could not locate them in the vast throng.

He glanced at his colonel, wondering if he were not frightened among so many Indians. But Clark looked as if he were master of the entire council. Fear was not a part of George Rogers Clark's character; and since the Indians had asked him to come to the council, he waited for them to speak.

After a few minutes a tall, erect, haughty chief, dressed in a handsome buffalo robe, came forward to stand directly in front of Colonel Clark. "Chief Long-Knife," he began, "we hope the Great Spirit has brought us together for good and that we may be received as friends. The bad bird British ordered us to attack your countrymen."

He turned and motioned for one of his tribesmen to bring something to him. When the Indian brought him a bloody belt, some red wampum and two British flags, the chief threw them to the floor and stomped upon them.

"We have received these emblems of war from the bad bird British and now we hope peace with you will take the place of the bloody belt of war." Then the chief walked back to his people. Other chiefs came up asking for peace. Even the Winnebagos came up and offered the peace pipe to Colonel Clark.

He waved them away, however, because he knew it

was best to keep the Winnebagos in suspense for a while about the fate of their Stinker relatives still in chains. Then he told all chiefs who had made speeches that he would consider their offer and give them an answer the next day. He left the council with his staff, and all the townspeople and Jim.

The next morning after the council fires were kindled anew, George Rogers Clark gave his answer to the waiting Indians. He told them why the Long-Knives were at war with the British, and that the British had become so weak they were forced to hire Indians to fight for them. He also told them the French king, father of all their French friends, had also joined the Long-Knives against the British.

Finally he said, "Now you can judge who is right, the Long-Knives or the British. Here is the bloody belt of war, here the white belt of peace. Take the one you please. Behave like men though, and choose the one you wish.

"I do not want you to give me an answer until you have

time to counsel. We will part, and when you are ready, if the Great Spirit will bring us together again, let us prove ourselves worthy by speaking and thinking with one heart and one tongue." Then Colonel Clark and his group left the council, not returning until the Indians sent for him.

They had assembled with their peace pipes, and many chiefs made flowery speeches about their intended friendship with the Long-Knives. Later they smoked their peace pipes and offered them to Clark, who went through the pipe-smoking ceremony with them.

Jim Hudson knew Indians did not always keep their word; how he hoped Colonel Clark knew it, too.

These council meetings went on for days until Jim grew weary of attending them. One morning, however, he was surprised to see two stalwart young Winnebagos present themselves in front of Colonel Clark, then fall to the ground and cover themselves with a blanket.

Jim did not know what to make of this and looked questioningly at the colonel. George Rogers Clark's face did not change expression as he waited to see what would happen next.

One of the Winnebago chiefs stepped forward; he explained that these two young men were offering themselves as a sacrifice to atone for what their Winnebago relatives had done at Clark's headquarters.

Colonel Clark did not reply at once, but kept staring at the blanket covering the two men. Jim and the rest waited anxiously, expecting the colonel to order the Winnebagos killed immediately, or at least to be cast into irons.

To everyone's amazement, Colonel Clark rose and ordered the two Indians to stand. Then he took each of them by the hand as brothers and introduced them to his officers and the Frenchmen sitting with his group. A loud murmur of approval arose from the surprised Indians. Still more surprising to Jim was Clark's order to free the Stinkers who had tried to kidnap him.

All during these meetings Jim had looked in vain for the Potawatomis with whom he had spent the winter; he wondered if they had ever arrived in Cahokia. The day after Clark had freed the Stinkers, Jim discovered Chief Minnemung and his clan sitting near the front of the assembly. For a moment he was afraid—would these Potawatomis try to capture him again? Then he glanced at Colonel Clark and realized he was safe where he was.

At this council meeting Big Gate, one of the great Potawatomi chiefs, spoke for the entire tribe, saying they were ready to sign a peace treaty with the Long-Knives. When the treaty was signed, Colonel Clark and his staff rose to leave. Suddenly Chief Minnemung barred his path.

"Big Long-Knife, chief of all the Long-Knives," Minnemung began, nodding toward Jim, "this boy ran away from our clan. I planned to adopt him as my own son."

Jim began to tremble when Colonel Clark turned to him, all the while pretending he had never known of Minnemung's plan. "Jim," he said sternly, "is this true?"

"Yes, sir," Jim stammered, "but I didn't want——"

Chief Minnemung gestured impatiently, as he interrupted Jim. "Big Long-Knife, I say Chief Minnemung no longer wants to adopt this boy. He not make good Potawatomi. He is Jim Long-Knife. Chief Minnemung is no longer interested in him. He now belongs to Big Long-Knife Clark."

Jim sighed in relief as Clark said gravely, "So be it, Chief Minnemung. I accept this boy as Jim Long-Knife." He extended his hand to the Potawatomi chief to seal their bargain.

Chief Minnemung shook hands with Clark without glancing at Jim. Then he walked proudly to his clan.

George Rogers Clark could be stern no longer. As he looked at Jim for a moment, his hazel eyes twinkled in fun. "I guess this makes you safe, Jim. You are now under my control and a real Long-Knife. Chief Minnemung has decreed it. Jim Long-Knife. That's a fine name for you."

Jim smiled. "Oh, sir, thank you. I'm so glad Chief Minnemung doesn't want me. I saw him sitting with the other Indians today, and I was afraid he might have his men take me prisoner again sometime."

Kaskaskia

Chapter VIII

A PEACEFUL INTERVAL

While Clark was counseling and making treaties with the different Indian tribes at Cahokia, he was also sending men on different missions throughout the western country.

For the most important mission he chose Father Gibault and Dr. Laffont, an influential citizen of Kaskaskia. They were to take a proclamation to the French settlers at Vincennes, asking them to renounce their fidelity to the British king, George III and swear allegiance to the Americans.

Since Father Gibault was well known and respected for his earlier good works among the people there and Dr. Laffont was a most persuasive man, the French settlers willingly took their oath of allegiance to the Americans.

Both men returned to Colonel Clark with this good news long before his negotiations with the Indians were completed. Then Clark dispatched Captain Helm to take charge of Fort Sackville at Vincennes.

Now that the three French villages, Kaskaskia, Cahokia and Vincennes were in American hands, about half of Clark's volunteers returned to their homes in Kentucky and Virginia. Those who stayed acted not only as guards for the American headquarters, but reinforced the French garrisons at Kaskaskia and Cahokia against possible Indian attack.

Jim didn't know how to occupy his time, now that Colonel Clark didn't seem to need him. One evening he decided to ask the colonel about it. "I have nothing to do here, Colonel Clark," he began. "I could go back to

Kentucky to see what's left of our farm. I wouldn't be afraid to stay there alone, sir, and I could start clearing more land."

Colonel Clark fidgeted in his chair. "I know you aren't afraid, Jim, but I wouldn't think of letting you go back alone. You'd be a perfect target for Indians. They haven't all signed treaties, remember. Even so, I don't trust these redskins too far. Now if your parents——"

"But, sir," Jim interrupted, "I don't know if my parents——"

"I know, lad. It'll be time enough for you to go back to your farm when we locate your father and mother. I have asked every man who has gone out from here to be on the lookout for the Hudsons. They are to ask in every settlement if any one has seen or heard of them. It's a slow sort of grapevine method, I know, but word gets around that way. We'll find them, Jim, some day."

Jim's blue eyes misted with tears. "Oh, Colonel Clark, you think of everything. No wonder you're such a good military leader."

"You can stay on at headquarters with me, Jim. That will give you a roof over your head and three meals a day." He stared at Jim for a moment and then grinned. "I'll have to find a buckskin outfit for you too, lad. Even if you are Jim Long-Knife, that ragged blue outfit you're wearing must be replaced."

Jim laughed. "These are the clothes the Potawatomis gave me. I have no others. The Shawnees took the ones my mother was taking to Harrodsburg."

"And you'll need some work to do, Jim, to keep you out of mischief."

"I can get a job, I'm sure. Willie told me he could get work for me with Monsieur Gabriel Cerré, the wealthy merchant here. Willie works for him."

Colonel Clark frowned. "Willie? Who's Willie?"

Jim seemed surprised. "Willie Watson, sir. The boy we found in the boat the night we took Kaskaskia."

Clark nodded. "To be sure. I remember you told me about him, but I didn't notice him that night. What does he do for Monsieur Cerré?"

"He sorts fur pelts and counts them. I saw him yesterday and he has already started the fall work."

"It sounds like a good job, Jim. Ask Willie to take you to see Monsieur Cerré."

"Yes, sir. I'll go over now and see Willie."

Jim started over to the fur depot to find Willie, but on the way he saw him coming. "Oh, Willie."

"Hello, Jim. Still running errands for Colonel Clark?"

"No. I guess my work with him is over. I was just coming to see if you could get me a job with Monsieur Cerré."

Willie smiled. "Sure. Just today the men were saying they needed another boy to sort pelts this fall."

"Can we go tomorrow?"

Willie shook his head. "There isn't going to be any work tomorrow. The men have to wait for some supplies coming up from New Orleans. I'll be glad to take you as soon as the depot opens again. I've just been talking to Father Gibault about getting the beeswax and honey from that bee tree I marked for him."

"Haven't you been across the river since that night?"

"No. You see Father Gibault thought it would be easier to get later in the fall. But since there's no work tomorrow he said I might go after it, if I could get someone to help me. Would you like to go along with me?"

Jim's eyes sparkled. "Sure, if Colonel Clark says I may."

"Come over about ten o'clock then. We can't go too early as we have to wait until most of the bees are out of the hive."

"I'll be there, Willie."

"Be sure to wear your moccasins—" Willie looked doubtfully at Jim's thin, worn clothes, "and you'd better get some buckskin clothes to wear. Bees can't sting through buckskin."

"All right. See you tomorrow."

Colonel Clark said Jim might go after the honey, but added he couldn't go unless they found some buckskin clothes for him to wear. He hunted through some of the supplies at headquarters and found a buckskin outfit.

When Jim arrived at Willie's house, Willie was ready and waiting for him. He handed Jim one large wooden bucket and carried another himself. "We'll put the honey and wax in these buckets," Willie explained. Then he picked up a gaily colored cloth bundle.

The two boys put out in one of Father Gibault's boats and soon crossed the Kaskaskia River, landing near the house which Clark had surrounded the night he made his march on Kaskaskia.

Willie moored the boat to a tree along the bank. Then they started out to find the tree Willie had marked with Father Gibault's initials. They wandered quite a way before Willie suddenly cried, "See, Jim, there it is!" He pointed to a tree with a large fork high above the ground.

Jim also saw the initials F. G. on the trunk; these Willie had carved the day the Long-Knives had found him in the boat. "Why did you put Father Gibault's initials there, Willie?"

"Why, to show the honey belonged to Father Gibault. No one will steal honey from a marked tree," Willie explained as he untied his cloth bundle. Out tumbled two blue *capots* or cloaks with hoods, two small scarfs and two pairs of mittens. Then he took out a long, sharp knife from the pocket of one of the *capots*. "Now we'll get dressed to tackle the bees."

Jim picked up the larger *capot* and tried it on. "I can't wear this, Willie. It's too small."

Willie had already put on his *capot* and adjusted its hood over his head. "You can't? Say, you're bigger than I thought. That's my mother's *capot,* but I guess you need a man-sized one. Just put the hood over your head and let the cloak fly," he suggested as he tied a scarf over his face.

Jim looked at the *capot* dubiously. "Why are we wearing all this stuff anyway, Willie?"

"To keep the bees from stinging us, of course."

"We'll smother, Willie, and we can't see with the scarfs over our faces."

Willie nodded. "That's right. I'm a stupid ox not to think of that. Well, I'll fix it." He picked up the knife and cut two slits in each scarf. "Now we have peepholes. Put one on, and the mittens too, Jim. If the bees are in a bad mood, they can't sting us through the buckskin and these winter clothes."

Jim put them on and then asked, "Now what do we do?"

"I'll climb up and start cutting the honey and wax away. It's up there in a deep hole in the fork of the tree. You put your bucket at the base of the tree and I'll try to drop the honey and wax into it. This is a beautiful day, so maybe most of the bees will be gone from their hive."

Jim watched as Willie climbed the tree. What a ridiculous sight he was, with the blue *capot* flapping against his skinny legs.

Willie thrust the long knife into the hole and began turning it slowly around and around. Only a few bees emerged and buzzed around his blue hood.

"Fix the bucket, Jim," Willie called as the honey began oozing down the tree.

Jim put his bucket under the tree and began slapping

at a few bees that were buzzing all around him.

"Don't fight them, Jim. It makes them angry. Just let them buzz and I don't think they'll sting you."

Soon Willie had rolled out so much honey and beeswax that his bucket would not hold it all. When both buckets were filled, Willie came down from the tree. "Now you carry one and I'll carry the other."

Quite a bit of honey had trickled down the tree, so the bees stayed behind, instead of following Willie and Jim.

As the boys walked back through the woods, Willie looked admiringly at Jim. "I didn't realize you're so much larger than I am," Willie said. "Why, you're as tall as lots of men. How old are you?"

Jim smiled. "I guess I grew a lot while I was with the Potawatomis. I'm thir— why, Willie, I'm fourteen now. I forgot all about my birthday this year. But no wonder, I was fourteen the day after we captured Kaskaskia the fifth of July."

Willie stood as tall as he could. "Why, I'm almost as old as you, Jim. I'll be fourteen the second of January."

Jim was almost a head taller than Willie. He looked down at the younger boy and smiled. "You will? I thought you were about twelve."

"I may be short, but I can do lots of things that men can't do," Willie replied.

"Oh, I'm sure of that," Jim agreed.

Father Gibault was delighted with the amount of honey and wax that the boys brought back, and gave half the honey to Jim for Colonel Clark and his men. When Willie told him Jim would like to work alongside of him, Father Gibault said he would put in a good word for him to Monsieur Cerré.

A few days later Jim went with Willie to the fur depot to see Monsieur Cerré. The merchant put him to work with Willie, sorting and counting the pelts which Indians and French *voyageurs* had brought into Kaskaskia during the fall and winter.

Jim and Willie became the best of friends, spending many long evenings together either at Willie's house or at Colonel Clark's headquarters. Jim taught him to play his drum; Willie was such an apt pupil and so filled with rhythm that he soon played as well as Jim. In return Willie taught Jim all the gay lilting French songs he knew.

Jim enjoyed living in Kaskaskia; if his parents had been with him, he would have willingly spent the rest of his life among the French. They were a gay light-hearted people, always ready to stop work and have fun.

The men played cards endlessly on the outdoor galleries until winter winds drove them indoors. There were many church festivals to attend, dances for the boys to watch and always excellent food. At Christmas time there were many gay parties given for the French citizens and Clark's soldiers.

On New Year's Day of 1779 came the best day of all. The whole village turned out in its finest clothes to call at the homes of well-to-do folk.

And what a colorful procession they made; the men wore silken hose and bright silver shoe buckles, their richly trimmed coats open to show their fancy, embroidered waistcoats; the women dressed in feathered finery

imported from France by way of New Orleans and the
Mississippi River. Ordinary French settlers wore buckskin trousers and long colored cotton shirts belted in by
colored bead sashes tied behind, and topped by the familiar blue *capots*. Now and then there appeared in the
crowd a soldier in an ancient French uniform, or a *voya-
geur* in his leather ruffled shirt and brightly colored cap
with bobbing tassel.

Jim found life good in Kaskaskia until one afternoon
in late January. On the twenty-ninth day of the month
Jim came home from work and met a well-dressed gentleman just leaving Colonel Clark's headquarters. Jim
wondered who this man was.

As Jim walked into the house, George Rogers Clark
was pacing the floor and running his hand nervously
through his shock of red hair. He didn't even see Jim
come in, but continued to pace back and forth. Jim took
off his coat and hung it in the closet. Then he came back
into the large living room.

"Is something wrong, Colonel?"

Clark stopped and turned toward Jim. "Hello, Jim. I didn't hear you come in. Yes, I've just received some bad news."

"From the gentleman who was leaving as I came into the house?"

"Oh, did you see him? That was Francis Vigo, a Spanish merchant from St. Louis. I had asked him to see about Captain Helm's supplies, since he was going on a merchandising trip to Vincennes."

"Yes, sir." Jim waited, seeing Colonel Clark was quite upset.

"I've had no word from Captain Helm for a long time," Clark continued. "And that's not like Helm, so I was a bit uneasy. Vigo told me that he himself was captured and taken to Fort Sackville. There he was confronted by Lieutenant Governor Hamilton. You see, Jim, Hamilton captured Fort Sackville on the seventeenth of December and Captain Helm is now his prisoner. The British are again in control of Fort Sackville and Vincennes."

Jim gasped. "Do you mean Hamilton from Detroit?"

"The very same. He took all of Vigo's merchandise from him and wouldn't release him until Vigo promised not to return to Kaskaskia on his way home to St. Louis." Clark smiled wryly. "Vigo kept his promise too. He went home to St. Louis, then came over here immediately to tell me about Helm."

Jim looked puzzled. "What does it mean for us now that Hamilton is in Vincennes?"

"Vigo told me Hamilton plans to attack Kaskaskia as soon as the weather permits, some time in the spring. He's supposed to have an army of eight hundred men, counting the Indians and his prisoners."

"Eight hundred!" Jim gasped. There weren't eight hundred people in the two towns of Kaskaskia and Cahokia.

Colonel Clark resumed his pacing back and forth as though he had forgotten Jim. After a time he stopped suddenly. "Attack at once, Jim. That's what we'll do." He brought his fist down hard in the palm of his hand.

"It's our only chance. We'll attack Hamilton now when he thinks it's impossible. But we'll make it."

Jim's blue eyes sparkled reflecting Clark's confidence. "Yes, sir. What can I do to help you now?"

"Run to Father Gibault's and ask him if he will come to my headquarters at once. Then see if you can find Captain Charleville and tell him to report to me immediately. But do not tell them or anyone else what I have just told you. Do not even mention Vigo's visit."

"No, sir, I won't."

Colonel Clark then called one of his officers who had been asleep upstairs. "You," he nodded toward the man as soon as he appeared, "ride to Cahokia tonight. Tell Captain McCarty to bring his company back from Cahokia immediately."

"Yes, sir," replied the officer.

Jim dashed out of the house toward Father Gibault's, while Clark's officer mounted his horse and set off at a gallop for Cahokia.

Father Gibault and Captain Charleville returned to

headquarters with Jim almost immediately. George Rogers Clark told them the bad news of Vincennes and what he had in mind to do.

Father Gibault looked grave for a few minutes and then said, "Colonel Clark, I'm not a military man, but I think your plan of attack is good. God willing, you will make it."

Captain Charleville sat forward in his chair. "Colonel Clark, there aren't many of your Virginia volunteers here now, but I'm sure I can raise a company among the villagers."

Colonel Clark nodded. "We'll have to have volunteers, Charleville. I don't have more than eighty men, including the men under Captain McCarty at Cahokia. I've sent for him to return with them. We can't do anything more until morning, gentlemen. Thank you for responding so quickly."

"I'll have a full company raised before sunset tomorrow, sir," Captain Charleville promised.

Chapter IX

THROUGH THE DROWNED LANDS

The next morning Father Gibault rang the church bell, signaling all people to assemble at the church. Immediately the villagers came streaming out of their houses or stores. Colonel Clark and Jim waited outside for them to appear. Jim had brought his drum, and played it loudly to attract their attention.

Willie Watson came running to the church; when he saw Jim, he pushed through the crowd to him.

"What's all the excitement, Jim? What's happened?" Willie asked breathlessly.

Jim didn't lose a drumbeat as he replied, "Wait and find out, Willie. Colonel Clark is going to talk to the people."

As soon as everyone was quiet, Father Gibault told them that Colonel Clark had an important message for them. Then Colonel Clark told them that even now Hamilton was in command of Vincennes and was planning to attack Kaskaskia as soon as the weather permitted.

Before the citizens could recover from this shock, Clark had outlined his plan of an immediate march on Vincennes and a surprise attack on Fort Sackville. He said he would need volunteers to help build a supply boat he would send ahead for his army.

"I'll help. I'll help," came the cry of the men from every quarter.

"And we'll help, too," the women cried. "We'll make flags for your army. You'll need banners to carry."

Colonel Clark smiled and nodded. "Those of you who will help with the boat and supplies, step over on this side.

And you who will volunteer to go to Vincennes, sign up with Captain Charleville."

The men quickly made their choices, and Jim began to play his drum again to interest the men in joining Captain Charleville's company.

"Jim," asked Willie, who had stood quietly up to now, "are you going to Vincennes?"

"Of course, Willie. I haven't asked Colonel Clark, but he'll be needing a drummer, I know."

"If you're going, I am, too," Willie said, excitement making his voice shrill. "I think my mother has a rifle which belonged to my father. I can take it with me."

Jim looked doubtfully at Willie. "Can you fire a rifle?"

Willie shook his head. "No, but I can learn."

Jim grinned. "It takes a lot of practice, Willie, but I've an idea. If you'll let me have your father's rifle, I'll let you take my drum. You can play it well, and I've had experience with rifles. My father taught me to use one."

Willie smiled. "Will you, Jim? Sure—you can have the rifle."

"I don't think we'd better say anything to Colonel Clark until it's time to go," Jim cautioned. "He might think of an excuse to keep us from going with him."

"All right, Jim. Mum's the word, but I'll manage to get the rifle."

By nightfall Captain Charleville had raised his company of Kaskaskia volunteers. The women were so enthusiastic about the undertaking that they worked furiously for the next two days, making flags of various colors and designs. When they were presented to Colonel Clark, he didn't know what he would do with so many flags. But he thanked the ladies gravely and packed their gift with the army supplies.

On the third of February Captain McCarty arrived from Cahokia with his volunteers. That same day the men finished work on the riverboat, which Clark had named the *Willing*. They had made it into a warship equipped with armament of two four-pounders and four swivels. It required a crew of forty men to man, and Clark put Captain John Rogers in charge of it.

He ordered Rogers to go down the Kaskaskia and Mississippi Rivers to the Ohio and ascend the Ohio and Wabash Rivers; then he was to take his station thirty miles below Vincennes and wait there for further orders. The next day Captain Rogers and his crew set out on the warship with supplies, stores and ammunition.

At three o'clock in the afternoon of February fifth, Clark's army was ready to march. Jim had had to talk long and hard to get Clark's permission to go with the troops; he had made no mention of Willie. But Willie stood beside Jim, carrying his father's rifle, which protruded above his head.

As the army, one hundred-thirty men strong, stood waiting, Father Gibault made a little talk to the men and gave them his blessing and absolution. All the women and men not able to go with Clark were on hand to bid the troops good-bye and wish them Godspeed.

George Rogers Clark rode in front on a magnificent stallion, followed by his officers, also mounted. Jim Long-Knife Hudson, wearing an ill-fitting buckskin suit and beating his drum, stepped out proudly. Willie Watson dropped back to the rear of the second company, fearing Colonel Clark would see him and send him home because of his age and size.

The rest of the men, clad in worn buckskin trousers and hunting shirts, swung out jauntily, their heads held high. Some carried rifles and some tomahawks, since there weren't enough rifles for everyone. A motley array —Clark's pioneer army, and at the same time a magnificent column of spirited soldiers.

The whole of the flat Illinois country between Kaskaskia and Vincennes was freezing water and half-frozen mud. Two hundred and forty miles lay between the army and Vincennes, but the men bravely started out. By nightfall, however, they had covered only three miles. It was rainy and drizzly, so they spent an uncomfortable night without tents or shelter of any kind. The next day they remained in camp.

That night Colonel Clark spied Willie Watson for the first time. "Willie!" he cried, "what are you doing here?"

Willie trembled but stood his ground. "I'm marching with you to take Fort Sackville, sir," he replied.

Clark shook his head. "You're too young, Willie, for this trip. If I had seen you earlier, you would have remained at home."

Willie grinned mischievously. "Yes, sir. I've taken pains to stay out of your sight, sir. I was afraid you wouldn't let me come along. And I'm fourteen years old, as old as Jim Hudson. I brought my father's rifle too."

Clark smiled and then shook his head. "I admire your spirit, Willie. Can you fire your rifle?"

Willie shook his head slowly. "No, sir, I can't. But Jim is going to take my rifle and I'll play his drum."

Colonel Clark looked grave. "Since it's too late to send you home, Willie, I guess you'll just have to stay."

Willie smiled. "Oh, sir, thank you. I'll make it. You won't regret my coming, sir."

The next day the soldiers marched for nine hours, then pitched camp in a square on the driest ground they could find, putting their baggage in the center.

As they continued through succeeding days they marched sometimes through water up to their armpits. They had to hold rifles and powder high above their heads to keep them dry.

In desperation Clark and his officers dismounted and piled the baggage on their horses. The animals struggled along through the water with the men.

If any men happened to see any wild game, Colonel Clark gave them time to shoot it. Now and then they bagged a deer and on the twelfth of February they sighted a herd of buffalo.

"Here, Willie," Jim called, "take my drum and give me your rifle. Maybe I can get a buffalo."

Willie handed over the rifle, as Jim noticed with satisfaction it was exactly like his father's. He dashed out with two soldiers to shoot one of the buffalos. He went as close as he dared to the herd, took careful aim and fired. His buffalo dropped immediately as did several others which the men shot. In a few minutes they had dragged the buffaloes over toward the fires.

"Good boy, Jim," Willie said, clapping him on the back excitedly. "We'll eat plenty tonight."

Clark's army did eat a good meal and had entertainment afterward. Willie and Jim sang many of the songs they had learned together, and took turns playing the drum. Willie also danced a strange mixture of French and Indian dances until he was exhausted.

That evening the two boys helped boost the morale of Clark's army more than anyone else save the colonel himself. Colonel Clark was quick to give them credit. "We could never have made it this far, boys," he said, "without your music and dancing."

The boys were exhausted from their performance; Jim was too tired to say a word. But Willie grinned at Colonel Clark and said, "I told you, sir, you wouldn't regret letting me come with you."

During their first six days this remarkable army marched over one hundred and seventy-four miles, averaging twenty-eight miles a day. The hardest part of the trip, however, lay before them——the sixty-three miles to

Vincennes. They would have four rivers to cross—two branches of the Little Wabash, the Embarrass and the Great Wabash, all of them now swollen by floods.

When the army reached the two Little Wabash branches, normally three miles apart, the men were stunned to see a sheet of water almost five miles across, with no dry banks or channels for either branch in sight. The shallowest place was about three feet deep; what the greatest depth was, no man knew.

Colonel Clark ordered his soldiers to halt while he considered what to do. For a few minutes he gazed at the great expanse of water, then ordered some of the men to build a pirogue. This took only a day to build. Then he ordered a few others to explore these drowned lands and if possible, find a dry camping spot on the far bank of the second branch. Once they found a trail, they marked it with blazes on all trees above the waterline.

But how to get the loaded pack horses across both branches of the river? The horses could wade to the first channel easily enough, but when in deep water they would have to swim, and they could not swim with their heavy packs. Once again Colonel Clark solved his new problem. He had his men build a scaffold in a shallow spot beyond the second river bank.

When this was finished, the men unloaded the horses and moved the baggage over to the scaffold in their pirogue. Then they swam the horses through both channels, reloading the animals at the scaffold. They also ferried any ill, weak soldiers across both river branches.

As Colonel Clark himself plunged into the water, he expected the rest of his army to follow him along the tree-blazed route. But the men hung back, complaining they were already cold and wet enough without wading another five miles.

Suddenly Willie Watson, seeing Colonel Clark floundering through the water alone, seized Jim's drum and started into the water, beating the drum as hard as he could. "Come on, you," he called, beating a terrific roll. Jim plunged in right behind Willie, holding his rifle high above his head.

Soon the water was up to Willie's armpits. He pushed the drum down and sat on it, floating along and paddling the water with his drumsticks. "Come on, you fellows," he called. "Somebody give me a push."

A French sergeant, almost six and a half feet tall, charged into the water, scooped up Willie and his drum, put him on his shoulders and shouted, "Advance!"

Willie's courageous antics turned the trick for Colonel Clark. While Willie played and sang at the top of his lungs, the rest of the soldiers waded into the water and did not turn back, though in some places the water came up to their chins. But no dry spot could be found, so they had to spend the night in shallow water without food.

Somehow they continued to march through the ice-cold drowned lands until they had crossed the Embarrass and Wabash Rivers. Here the men in their soaking wet clothes were more discouraged than ever. This was the place where the *Willing* was supposed to be waiting for them. The warship, however, had not arrived.

The next day the camp awakened to a dull, boom.

"What's that?" Willie cried, poking Jim who lay beside him.

"I don't know," Jim mumbled. "Sounded like guns, didn't it?"

One soldier overheard the boys and said, "Colonel Clark said those were the British morning guns at Fort Sackville."

"Why, we're almost there," Jim cried, jumping up and stretching.

"Almost there!" sneered another soldier. "Take a look at that water."

"Where are we?" Willie asked, rubbing the sleep out of his eyes.

"About nine miles below Vincennes on the banks of the Great Wabash!" a nearby soldier exclaimed. "But how we'll ever get across that flood water I don't know." Several more men began to complain, and some even muttered about going home.

Jim and Willie looked around and saw Captain McCarty's men cutting down poplar trees.

"Come on, Willie," Jim said. "Let's see what they're going to do with those trees."

The boys went over to help drag the poplars to a dry area where the men could build canoes. They worked all day and by evening had finished two. Meanwhile the boys saw two more drifting aimlessly on the flood waters, so they waded out and captured them. Now Colonel Clark had four canoes to ferry his army over some of this vast expanse of river.

The next morning it was raining again and the water was still quite cold. Though the soldiers still had had nothing to eat, the stronger ones began ferrying the troops over to a small hill called Bubbie. From here they waded to a larger hill, clutching trees and bushes in the water to steady themselves. The canoes went alongside to watch for any sick men.

Those who were able built fires on the opposite side of the river and marched the exhausted men up and down in front of the fire to revive them.

At last they reached Warrior's Island, a dry spot of

about ten acres. From here Clark planned to attack Fort Sackville. The men had to rest, however, before he could order the attack.

A day or two later, some of Clark's scouts brought two Indian squaws and two half-grown boys into camp and presented them to him.

"What do I want with these people?" Clark demanded. "I haven't anything to feed to my own men, to say nothing of four prisoners."

"That's it, sir," one scout replied. "They had food in their canoe. It was filled with kettles, tallow, corn and half a quarter of buffalo meat. We have it here, but what shall we do with these Indians?"

"Food!" cried several of the men near the colonel. "Where?"

"Make some buffalo stew for the men immediately," Clark ordered. He looked at the trembling Indians. "I guess we'll have to take these prisoners to Vincennes with us."

Just at this moment Jim and Willie came up to the

colonel. When Jim saw the Indians, he stopped and stared as if he didn't believe his own eyes. Then he dashed over to the taller Indian boy. "Wahbunou!" he cried. "What are you doing here?"

Wahbunou tried to smile, but was too frightened to talk. He just grabbed Jim and clung to him.

George Rogers Clark looked at Jim in amazement. "Jim, do you know this boy?"

"Oh, sir," Jim cried, "this is Wahbunou, my Potawatomi friend that I told you about."

Colonel Clark looked keenly at the boy and then at Jim. "Is this the boy who did not tell his people about seeing the Long-Knives marching that summer afternoon?"

"Yes, sir."

Clark smiled at the Indian boy. "Well then, Wahbunou, I am sorry we had to take your food. But my men have had nothing to eat for several days. You are no longer a prisoner of Chief Long-Knife. All four of you are free to take your canoe and return home."

Wahbunou did not understand all that Colonel Clark said to him, but when Jim interpreted, the Indian boy nodded his head and smiled.

George Rogers Clark shook hands with Wahbunou and said, "If you will come to Fort Sackville in a few days I'll pay you for your food. Unfortunately, I have nothing to give you for it tonight."

Wahbunou nodded again, spoke to his Indian companions and motioned for them to follow him. They found their canoe and paddled rapidly away.

Meanwhile the men were busy making buffalo stew. When it was ready the weakest men were fed first. Though there wasn't enough stew to go around, it revived many exhausted soldiers and improved the spirit of all the soldiers.

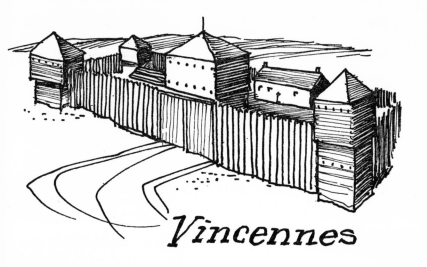

Vincennes

Chapter X

CAPTURE OF VINCENNES

From their camp the men could see the hundred cabins making up the town of Vincennes, and Fort Sackville over which the Union Jack was flying. If settlers in Vincennes turned toward Warrior's Island, they could see American soldiers; so George Rogers Clark employed a trick of war to make them think he commanded a large army.

While the men were resting after their taste of buffalo stew, two more of Clark's scouts came into camp bringing a very frightened Frenchman from Vincennes. They said they had found him lurking near the camp. Willie and Jim had been sitting near the colonel and could hear everything he said to the Frenchman.

Clark spoke sternly to the man cowering in front of him. "I will permit you to go into town under certain conditions. First you are to alert all French inhabitants and tell them we will take Vincennes tonight. They are to stay in their houses, keep quiet and not to let any one at Fort Sackville know of our presence. Oh, yes, and tell them to have a fine supper ready for us."

"Yes, sir," the man replied. "And to think you've marched all the way from Kentucky!"

Clark did not correct the man's guess about Kentucky. He merely said, "Now you may go, but do not go near the fort." As the Frenchman hurried to Vincennes to deliver his message, Colonel Clark watched through his field glass to see that he did not go to the fort.

About sunset Clark ordered his army to assemble. When they were in their respective companies, with Jim and Willie in front, Colonel Clark said, "I ask just one thing of all of you—OBEDIENCE. Absolte OBEDIENCE."

"Yes, sir," every man replied.

Clark turned to Jim and Willie. "You boys bring out the flags which we brought from Kaskaskia. We have good use for them now."

The boys went over to the small stock of supplies they had succeeded in bringing through the water, and took out the flags. These had been so well packed they were not even damp. There were twenty-four in all.

"Each officer is to have a pair of flags mounted on poles," Clark said.

The officers mounted several flags as Clark had directed. Willie and Jim wondered what they would do with the rest.

"See that small hill between us and the town?" Clark pointed to a hill about halfway to Vincennes. "You are to march your men around and around that hill, every sixth man carrying a flag so far as possible. Thus you will give the effect of many divisions, each carrying its flag, to anyone watching from Vincennes. When I give the order, you march around that hill until dark. Then I will issue your orders for the night."

Colonel Clark led the line of march, followed by Willie Watson with the drum, Jim Hudson, Captain McCarty and the first of the color bearers. They marched around and around the hill in plain view of the townspeople. Should anyone be watching, he might easily assume that George Rogers Clark had at least a thousand men at his command.

Finally night fell. Tension was mounting among the men. Now, now was the time for attack. How many men did Hamilton have? Had this army come all through the drowned lands to suffer defeat? Never, while they drew breath.

Such thoughts were in the mind of every man when Colonel Clark suddenly snapped them to attention.

"Lieutenant Baily," he ordered, "take fourteen of your best men and begin firing on the fort as soon as we have reached Vincennes. Then cease firing for a few minutes and laugh loudly as though you were firing for amusement."

The lieutenant stepped forward and called out fourteen men.

Colonel Clark went on. "I will lead the rest of this army to the heights behind Vincennes and enter the upper part of town. The sentinels on the stockade walls won't be able to see us, because part of the town lies between our line of march and their garrison."

Then he set out with the main army toward Vincennes, while Lieutenant Baily marched his fourteen men toward the stockade.

Jim and Willie, marching with the main army, became so excited they could scarcely set one foot after the other. In no time at all Clark's army took possession of the main street and posted guards. Scarcely anyone was in sight because of Clark's order for the people to remain in their houses. Jim was assigned to guard duty; Willie went with Colonel Clark on his rounds through the town.

In a little while Willie came hurrying back to Jim.

"Jim," he cried. "The people have supper ready for us. We're going to take turns eating. Colonel Clark said he'd send a man to relieve you shortly, and you're to come with me."

Just at this moment there was a burst of rifle fire, then the sound of raucous laughter.

"Our men have begun the attack, Willie," Jim cried, peering into the black night. "We'll soon take Vincennes and the fort."

There was, however, no answering fire from the fort. In a few minutes another volley of shots rent the air.

"Let's go nearer to the fort, Jim, and see what's going on."

Jim shook his head. "I can't, Willie. I'm on guard here, remember."

After another burst of fire by the Americans, there was a sudden, answering roar from the guns inside the fort.

Just at this moment Colonel Clark appeared with a man to relieve Jim. "You boys eat your supper. Report back here when you've finished, Jim," Clark said, and

went on to direct the firing which was now continuous.

"Come on, Jim. I know where we're supposed to go." Willie led the way to one of the villagers' homes, where seven or eight soldiers were just finishing their meal.

"Come in, boys," called a rosy-cheeked woman. "There is plenty of food for all of you."

The boys sat down to a bountiful dinner of roast duck, the best meal they had eaten since their buffalo feast many days ago. While they were eating, the woman kept staring at Jim. Finally she said, "Soldier, have I seen you before? There's something very familiar about your face."

Jim looked blankly at her. "I don't know, ma'am. I don't recall ever having seen you."

Still she looked at him. "It's sure queer. You remind me of someone. I can't quite figure—say, what's your name? Mine's Jeanne Duval."

Jim smiled. "Sometimes I'm called Jim Long-Knife. The Indians gave me that name. But my real name's Jim Hudson."

"Hudson!" Jeanne exclaimed, her voice shrill with excitement. "And where's your home?"

Jim shook his head. "I haven't any home now except with Colonel Clark. I used to live in Kentucky."

"Kentucky, you say. I wonder if you—"

The roar of cannon from Fort Sackville cut off her words. Jim and Willie jumped up. "Thank you, ma'am, for the good dinner. We can fight better now," Jim said, as they started out the door.

"When the fighting's over, come back here, Jim. Come back for sure."

"All right," Jim replied, "if I'm alive."

The boys made their way back to Jim's post and found it in the thick of the fighting. American soldiers were pouring the hottest fire possible into the fort.

"Look, Willie," Jim said as he got his rifle ready, "look at those gaps in the stockade."

Just then the British poked an artillery piece out of a porthole, while the Americans sent a shower of well-directed balls into it.

"Hurrah!" cried Willie, "got some British that time."

The intense firing from both sides went on until about four o'clock in the morning. Then Colonel Clark withdrew all his troops save a few observation parties, and the firing ceased.

About nine o'clock George Rogers Clark sent a flag of truce into the fort with a message to Hamilton asking him to surrender immediately. This Hamilton refused to do and the firing began anew. But three hours later Hamilton sent out a flag asking for a three-days' truce. Clark refused, but offered to have a conference with Hamilton in the church at once.

While Clark waited for his answer, everyone outside the fort, French and Americans alike, watched the fort gate to see what would happen. Willie and Jim were in the front row, waiting as impatiently as the rest.

"Jim!" Willie cried. "Look! The gate is opening."

And indeed it was. Out came a dignified man in the striking red uniform of a British colonel of regulars, a handsome Indian and a grinning American.

"That man in red must be Hamilton himself," Willie whispered.

"And there's Captain Helm!" exclaimed Jim. "You know he's been Hamilton's prisoner since last December."

The three men walked on to the church. There they were met by George Rogers Clark and Captain Bowman. All of them went into the church to hold their conference.

The villagers all began talking at once, wondering what would happen next. The American soldiers relaxed a little, but still held their rifles.

As Willie and Jim started to walk up the street, a woman ran out from the crowd calling to them. "Boys! Jim Hudson."

Jim turned and recognized Jeanne Duval. She was calling and beckoning to him. "Come with me, Jim. To my house." She nodded toward Willie. "You may come too, lad."

"I can only stay a minute, ma'am," Jim replied, glancing back at the church. "Colonel Clark might want me."

"All right. Just come on." She hurried on ahead and rushed into her house. When the boys appeared she said, "Sit down a minute. I'll be right back." Then she disappeared out the back door.

Willie shook his head. "What kind of business is this, Jim? Do you suppose it's a trap?"

Jim laughed. "I don't think so, Willie. After all we aren't such important people in Clark's army. She's probably going to feed us again."

In a few moments she returned with a thin, tired-looking blond woman. Jim stared at her for an instant, then rushed over and swept her into his arms. "Ma! Ma!," he cried. "At last! I'd almost given up hope of finding you."

Ma Hudson was laughing and crying at the same time. "Jim, how you've grown! Why, you're a man! Jim dear, we knew you were alive and well in Kaskaskia. Captain Helm told Pa."

"Captain Helm? But he's a prisoner of Hamilton. And where is Pa?"

Ma looked worried. "I hope he's still alive in the fort. Pa and I are also Hamilton's prisoners. Pa's probably had to man the guns against the Americans."

"Against his own countrymen!" Jim gasped. "How do you happen to be outside the fort?"

Ma shrugged her thin shoulders. "Since there wasn't any place for women in the fort, the British put me in one of the French homes here. And the people have been good to me." She smiled at Jeanne Duval.

"She's been staying right next door," Jeanne explained. "That's why I was so excited last night when I saw you. You look so much like your ma, and when you told me your name, I was sure you were her boy."

"How did you get away from the Shawnees and reach Vincennes, Ma?"

Ma Hudson sighed. "We didn't get away from them, Jim. I think they intended to take us up north to Hamilton, but the snows came and they weren't able to get through to Detroit. It was a rugged winter, with not much to eat."

Jim frowned. "How did you and Pa get down here?"

"Last autumn the Shawnees heard Hamilton was marching south, so they rode to meet him and traded us for some guns and blankets. Hamilton brought us down here with other prisoners. I've been mending for Hamilton's soldiers and sewing some for the people here. Your pa has been helping repair the fort."

Jim had forgotten all about Willie while talking with his mother. Suddenly he remembered him and said, "Ma, this is my best friend, Willie Watson. He's from Kaskaskia."

Ma smiled at Willie. "I'm glad to know you, Willie. You must have wonderful people in Kaskaskia, because Jim looks so well."

"The same to you, ma'am," stammered Willie, bobbing his head.

"We'd better be getting back now, Ma," Jim said. "I'll see you when Hamilton surrenders. Don't worry about Pa. I'm sure he's all right and will be free as soon as Colonel Clark takes over here." Jim turned to Jeanne Duval.

"Thank you, ma'am, for all you've done for Ma and me."

When the boys returned to the American lines, the conference was over. No one was certain, however, that Hamilton would agree to the surrender terms. Colonel Clark took no chances of deception by the British; he posted guards in houses near the fort and patrols in town. The rest of his army slept on their rifles and got their first real rest in many days.

The next day, February 25, 1779, Hamilton sent Captain Helm to Colonel Clark with the signed articles of surrender. George Rogers Clark then drew up his army in two lines facing each other in front of Fort Sackville to await Hamilton. All of Vincennes gathered behind the American army to see the surrender.

Promptly at ten o'clock the wooden fort gate opened, and Lieutenant-Governor Hamilton led his well-drilled, scarlet-clad regulars of the King's regiment between the lines of the ragged American soldiers. Captain Helm, amidst loud hurrahs from the crowd, hoisted the American flag above Fort Sackville. Fort Sackville and Vin-

cennes were now in American hands, never to be surren-
dered again.

Hamilton's prisoners of war were also turned over to
Colonel Clark, among them Pa Hudson. When Jim spied
him in the group, he forgot all about his duty as a soldier
and rushed over to throw his arms around his father.

"Pa," he cried, "I knew I'd find you sometime."

His father hugged him hard. "Ma and I knew from
Captain Helm that you were safe in Kaskaskia, but we
didn't know when we could get to you."

When the celebrations and ceremonies of surrender
were over, George Rogers Clark dispatched a detail to
Virginia with Hamilton, his prisoner of war, and sent
home the French who had accompanied the British leader
from Detroit.

Then Clark looked over the stores and supplies in the
fort. In them he found much clothing which had been
sent from Detroit for the British troops. From this supply every man in Clark's army received new shirts, caps,
vests and trousers. These were most welcome gifts be-

cause the men wanted to be presentable when they returned in triumph to Kaskaskia.

The Indians near Vincennes must have heard about Clark's gifts, because early one morning several of them came to the fort to receive presents from Chief Long-Knife. Jim was helping to distribute these when he recognized Wahbunou in the group.

"Here's Wahbunou, Colonel Clark," he said as the Indian boy approached them.

Colonel Clark smiled and extended his hand to Wahbunou. "You've come to be paid for that buffalo meat and corn, I suppose. Well, boy, I'm glad to pay you. They saved our lives and made it possible for us to take Vincennes." The colonel himself looked through the supplies and brought out two magnificent blankets. "Can you use these blankets, Wahbunou?"

Wahbunou's eyes shone as he took the blankets. "These are very good, Chief Long-Knife. I have been paid plenty. I am glad my people could help Jim's people. Jim is my friend."

Jim took Wahbunou to one side. "My parents are here, Wahbunou," he said. "They were Hamilton's prisoners, but now they are free. Won't you stop and see them?"

Wahbunou beamed. "I'm glad you are with them. I can't stop now, but Wahbunou will see your mother when he comes to Vincennes again soon. Your mother was very kind to me." Then he turned and went back to the other Indians.

Before Colonel Clark led his men back to Kaskaskia, he took Willie Watson to make a call on the Hudsons. Pa Hudson wanted to return to his farm in Kentucky and asked Colonel Clark if he would advise going.

Clark was silent for a few minutes, then shook his head. "Not yet, Hudson. Why don't you stay here until summer? If everything is favorable then, you and your family can return to Kentucky. I'll be back in June as we intend to march on Detroit." Then he turned to shake hands with Jim.

"You've been a good soldier, Jim Long-Knife. They don't come any better than you. I'll say good-bye now and expect to see you when I return."

Jim's eyes misted as he said, "Thanks for everything, Colonel. I've learned a lot from you."

Willie had been unusually silent during the call. Now he said, "Good-bye, Jim. Take care of yourself. I'll miss you more——" his voice broke and he could not finish what he wanted to say.

Jim clapped Willie's shoulder affectionately. "Good-bye, Willie. You stay with Colonel Clark and the Long-Knives and you'll be all right. See you in June."

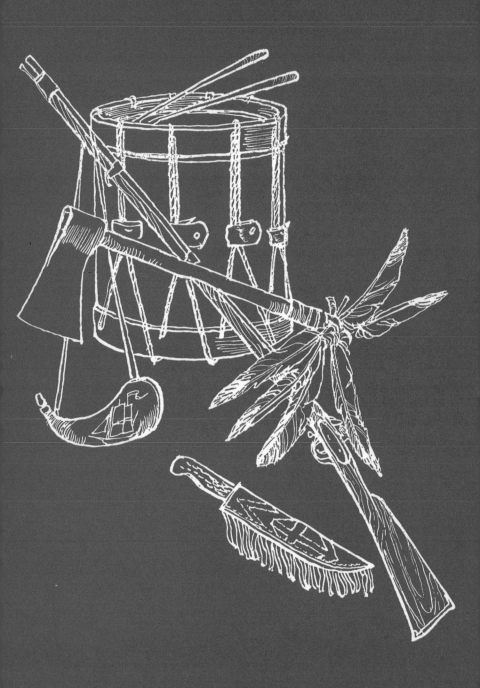